103 CURRENT TOPICS ON

ESSAYS, LETTERS & STORIES

FOR MIDDLE CLASSES

G. K. Gupta

MG BOOKS
NEW DELHI (INDIA)

103 CURRENT TOPICS ON

ESSAYS, LETTERS & STORIES

Published by

MG BOOKS

An Imprint of

MAANU GRAPHICS

MAANU GRAPHICS
(PUBLISHERS OF GENERAL BOOKS)
5FF, Ganpati Bhawan, 21 Ansari Road,
Darya Ganj, New Delhi-110002
Ph: 65285220, 64138266
E-mail : maanugraphics@yahoo.com
mgbooks.maanu@yahoo.com

ISBN 978-93-80078-18-2

Printed at
NEW Z. A. Printers, Delhi

CONTENTS

ESSAYS

LETTERS

STORIES

ESSAYS

A BIRTHDAY PARTY

Last Monday I attended a birthday party of my friend. It was his fifteenth birthday. He celebrated it with great pomp and show.

He had invited all his friends and relatives. The arrangement of party was done in hall of a hotel. I, along with other friends reached there in time.

His parents were standing at the door of the hall. They greeted all the guests arriving at the hotel. They greeted us and welcomed us in the party. We entered the hall and took our seat.

We were offered cold drinks and snacks. My friends Gagan was busy in meeting his relatives. Gagan saw us and came to meet us.

We wished him happy birthday and presented him the gift. He asked us to take cold drinks and enjoy ourselves. The guests kept on coming.

In late evening the cake cutting ceremony started. A big table was put in the centre of the hall. A huge cake was on the table. Gagan and his parents stood by the table.

All other relatives gathered there. Gagan blew off the candles and cut the cake. Everybody clapped and sang 'happy birthday to you'. Gagan gave a piece of cake to his mother and father. Every body wished him long happy life.

After this dinner started and we took our dinner. Music started playing dance songs. People started dancing on the dance floor. We also danced with Gagan for some time.

It was getting late. We decided to leave. We met Gagan and once again congratulated him on his birthday. We also congratulating his parents and took their leave.

It was a nice evening. We were feeling tired. We came back to our house late in the night.

☆☆☆

A COLD DAY IN WINTER

In hot countries, people generally welcome winter. But in cold countries, they consider it a cruel season. However, even in hot countries, winter sometimes seems cruel when it is unbearably cold.

This is how I felt on 28th January last. I had a disturbed sleep at night due to intense cold. As I woke up, I found the day no better.

I took courage to open the door of bed-room. A waft of biting cold greeted me and I began to shiver. I at once shut the door. It seemed that my hands and feet were becoming numb. I at once rushed to my bed and covered myself with the warm woollen quilt.

I asked my mother to prepare tea for me. She at once complied to my request and brought a cup of sizzling tea to me.

As I sipped hot tea, I got some relief. I took

courage to have a bath with luke-warm water. After the bath I again fell shivering with cold. Clouds of vapour were coming out of my mouth. Now, I took a cup of hot milk with my breakfast.

I went to school fully loaded with warm clothes but still feeling uneasy because of cold. The same was the condition of other children.

As I returned home we took meals in the dining room with doors all shut. We took hot pakoras with tea in the evening.

Then some guests arrived. More than anything else, the main topic of all the talk was cold.

As I sat for doing my homework, my hands refused to work properly because of cold. My mother switched on the room-heater. After a few minutes, the air in the room became warm and all of us heaved a sigh of relief.

The evening news bulletin said that it was the coldest day of the year.

☆☆☆

A HOT DAY IN SUMMER

The summer vacation had begun and I had to stay at home most of the time. My parents had decided to remain in Delhi all through the summer. I was extremely disappointed.

Delhi is known for its extreme climate and I began to dread the summer of Delhi. It becomes so not that one is not allowed to play outdoors.

There is always a risk of a sunstroke or heatstroke. Even if one plays in the evening the heat makes it impossible for anyone to enjoy the game. The worst months in Delhi are May and June.

It was the 25th June. I woke up late in the morning as usual. Most of my friends were away to hill stations and I was at a loose end. I didn't know what to do to keep myself pleasantly occupied the whole day.

Much against my mother's wishes, I decided to

go to the movie theatre all by myself. There was a good movie on at Plaza which is in Cannaught Place. I set out from home at 10.30 A.M. for the noon show.

In the scorching heat of mid-June. I set out on foot to get to the bus stop. After what seemed like a lifetime I reached the bus stop and found a shady comer to stand and wait.

It was almost ten minutes since I had been waiting for the bus to arrive. I began to feel faint in the heat. My thirst knew no bounds and I felt my throat gradually drying up. Finally the bus arrived and I found a window seat.

The journey was uncomfortable to say the least. There were people in the bus who were also suffering the effect of the intense heat. The bus was crowded which made it even more difficult for anyone to breathe fresh air. I thanked God when my stop arrived.

The line for the tickets was so long that I almost decided to go back home. The thought of getting bored at home kept me back and after spending half and hour of cursing and grumbling in the line I bought the ticket.

The movie started and after an hour there was a power failure. I cursed my luck and began to feel claustrophobic in the packed, hot, dark theatre.

The generators were set to work and soon the electricity was restored. I thanked God when I reached home after two hours. The comfort of my cool home brought life back into me.

☆☆☆

A JOURNEY BY A BLUELINE BUS

Travelling by a Blueline bus is an adventure for a young man and a trying experience for an old man. Formerly, it was only the fear of pick-pockets who could at the most liquidate one's pocket but in these changed times when terrorism is on the rise, travelling by a Blueline bus amounts to inviting danger or even death to oneself.

Who knows there may be a bomb under the seat which could blow the entire bus to pieces. But there is no escape from it as one has to travel long distances to reach work places and these Blueline buses are the cheapest mode of transport.

Once I had a bitter experience of a terrible journey by a Blueline bus. As soon as I reached the bus stop, I saw a long queue of passengers waiting anxiously for buses. The buses which came were already packed to full.

After too much jostling and pushing when I was able to get into it, I thanked my stars. But my sorrows did not end here. I had to wrestle with other fellow passengers to move to the front and adjust somewhere along with others.

Human beings were huddled together like suitcases in a luggage van and everyone was perspiring.

Whenever any seat was vacated by any passenger, people jumped at it to occupy it but only a lucky person used to get it after which he would look around with a smiling face as if he had got the throne of a king.

Whenever the driver applied brakes, the passengers fell upon one another. There were scenes of quarrels and disputes among men and women, which were warded off by clever people.

The conductor was asking the people to buy their tickets and cautioning them to examine under seats for any bomb.

At the next stop, I got down the bus. In this way,

my long journey by the bus came to an end, and by the time I reached my destination, I was tired and exhausted. My dress and shoes were spoiled but my limbs were atleast intact.

☆☆☆

A RAIL ACCIDENT

India has the second largest network of Railways in the world. The accidents are also very common on the railway track.

Some accidents take place because of some mechanical failure, but most of them are the result of some human error. Last week I observed a horrible railway accident. It was because of an error committed by the station master.

It so happened that I was there at the station in the second class waiting hall. I had to catch a train which was late. So, I was leisurely looking here and there.

A goods train was standing at the platform No. 2. Suddenly, it got a jolt and the bogies rushed fast in one direction. At first, I was surprised to see this, as no engine was fastened to the goods train.

I alongwith a large number of other people at once ran towards the platform and what a horrible sight we saw! The station master had given a wrong signal to a fast moving mail train such that it had rammed headlong into the stationary goods train.

The mail train virtually ran on the goods train. Its engine and two bogies were, as if riding the hind bogies of the goods train. We learnt that the engine driver of the mail train had lost his life. About two hundred passengers were killed. Many more were injured.

The news of the accident spread like wild fire. The people rushed to the spot. The injured were taken to hospitals. All the passengers were provided with water, milk, food and medicines.

Some effective steps for the safety of railway passengers should be taken.

★★★

A RAIL JOURNEY

My winter vacation had just begun when I received an invitation from my cousin to visit her at Lucknow. Due to official reasons, my parents offered me the chance to trave alone. I accepted.

There was nothing to fear as my father escorted me to my reserved berth and further, my uncle had confirmed to be at the station to receive me.

On Friday I boarded the Lucknow Mail from New Delhi railway station. It departed at 9.30 pm.

I waved as long as I could see my father and then monkeyed up to my reserved berth. I placed my small suitcase and a handbag in one corner and made myself comfortable. I had rented a pillow and a blanket and tucked myself cozily.

I looked around at the passengers near me. A

touring executive was on the berth at my level. On the four berths below me was a family. Parents and their two pretty daughters who soon became my friends. On the two berths across was a couple.

The compartment was full of activity for more than an hour. After people ate their dinner, they preferred to sleep. The Ticket Checker made his round. I did not have the need to watch other people around me.

My two friends, Renu and Ruchi, were a good company and together we three had an enjoyable time till we reached our destination. They too were visiting their cousin at Lucknow.

I joined Renu and Ruchi at the lower berth after their parents slept on the middle berths. We played card games and I learnt a few magic tricks from them. We discussed our studies and I was happy to know that Ruchi was of my age and in the same class. Renu was a year older.

They had bought some comics and they shared them with me. I had a packet of sweets which I happily shared with them. We could not continue for long as we sat in semi-lying position and our back ached. I moved to my berth.

I slept for some time. When I woke up the train had just moved out of Moradabad Station. My two friends were sleeping. I decided to take a round in the compartment.

The curtains were drawn and there was nothing much to be noticed. I returned to my berth. I was getting bored and restless. I forced myself to sleep again.

Hustle-bustle disturbed my sleep. I rubbed my eyes. I thought that the train was stationed at Bareilly. I got down and looked out of the window.

We had reached Kanpur. The executive had gone and people were heard directing each other to take care of the children and baggages. My friends woke up and so did their parents. I was introduced to Uncle and Aunty and when they heard about our night chats they seemed surprised.

We five drank tea and I shared my packed of biscuits. Our card game continued. Time passed. As we were drawing nearer to our destination the compartment was coming to life. Lest we forget later, we quickly exchanged our addresses. We even hoped to meet by chance in Lucknow.

The train was scheduled to reach the Lucknow Station at 7 am. We wished to be spared from unwanted delays.

Thankfully, the train moved into the station right on time. We looked out of the window to spot our respective Uncles. We did. At the station we took leave and I reached home to be greeted by an ever smiling cousin and a loving Aunt.

☆☆☆

A ROAD ACCIDENT

Accidents are very common in big cities as there are many modes of transport and roads are becoming narrow and overcrowded. We hear of them and read about them in newspapers almost daily.

Such accidents result in loss of life and material. These are caused by carelessness of drivers and their ignorance and negligence of traffic rules.

Once my brother and I decided to see a movie at Golcha Cinema at Daryaganj in Delhi. As we were getting late for the show, we began walking fast along the crowded road. All of a sudden there was a loud noise.

I saw a man rolling on the ground. He had been knocked down by a car. The car driver was driving at normal speed. He saw a lorry coming from the opposite direction. It was being driven rashly.

Since the car driver feared a collision, he tried to turn his vehicle aside, but his clutch wire gave way and the machine got out of control. It ran into a passerby and hit the pavement.

The man was seriously wounded. He sustained injuries on the head and face. His nose was bleeding and one his legs was badly bruised. A crowd gathered on the spot. The wounded man was rushed to a nearby hospital.

Some people started abusing and hitting the car driver. Some one tried to convince them that it was not his fault. It was just an accident.

Luckily, the victim was declared out of danger. His wounds were dressed and he was advised rest in bed to get over the shock.

The police also arrived at the place of the accident. The car as well as the lorry driver were taken to the police station. Their statements were recorded. The car driver was let off but the lorry driver was detained.

☆☆☆

A VILLAGE FAIR

Last week, I happened to visit Kotla which is a small village near Bareilly. My uncle who lives there had invited me.

It was my good luck that I reached the village when a famous local village fair was to be held the next day.

My uncle took me to the fair. It was being held just at the outskirts of the village. It covered an area of a few acres of land.

We heard noises of vendors and visitors quite a few metres before we reached the fair. As we reached closer and closer to the fair the noises were heard louder and louder.

We saw at the fair a great many makeshift shops and kiosks. There were all kinds of shops such as toy shops, cosmetics shops, jewellery shops, cassettes shops, general merchants shops and so many others. The greatest rush was seen at the sweet shops and small-time eateries.

Everywhere the village men and women with their children, all clad in gorgeous clothes were moving to and fro, some of them eating sweets or buns.

Others were taking snacks with tea. Cold drinks were in great demand. Young girls were buying colourful glass bangles. Children were pressing their parents to buy them toys.

In one corner, a snake-charmer was playing his flute while a black cobra was dancing in front of him. A large number of people gathered around him, were watching the cobra dance. In another corner a juggler was showing his tricks.

There were some other spots which attracted people's attraction. At one place there were going on lucky games. At another place wrestling bouts were being held. At yet another place, an astrologer was telling the people about their fate.

I was very happy. I took a cold drink. Then I bought a teddy bear and we returned home. I was bubbling with joy.

☆☆☆

AN IDEAL CITIZEN

We are all citizens of India and we are proud of being so, and that's a good idea, but the question is, are we all ideal citizens?

It is not easy to be an ideal citizen. An ideal citizen, as the term signifies, has and follows high ideals. What are the important ideals that an ideal citizen observes? Some of them can be noted easily.

An ideal citizen is a very useful member of society, not just by virtue of his profession, but also by virtue of his behaviour and attitude to society and country and to his neighbours.

Such a citizen does whatever is within his means to further the cause of democracy, security and justice.

He casts his own vote and that very honestly only to the party or candidate that he thinks genuinely deserves it. He also encourages others to cast their votes fairly and fearlessly to the candidates of their choice.

Such a citizen has a high civic sense. He does not waste water, food products or any kind of energy items such as gas, electricity, etc.

An ideal citizen renders yeoman's service in time of need. At the time of natural and national calamities, such as earthquakes, fires, floods, famines, terrorist attacks, riots, war, etc. an ideal citizen not only contributes liberally, but also does all kinds of social work that he can and all that selflessly.

An ideal citizen is a true patriot. He does not spread rumours. He is honest in paying his taxes. He is ready to lay down his life for his country.

He takes an active part in all national programmes such as literacy drive, pulse polio, malaria eradication, etc.

☆☆☆

DEEPAWALI

A festival plays a great role as it brings new joy and hope to the people. Of all the festivals I like Diwali. Diwali or Deepawali which means rows of lights is an important festival of the Hindus. It is celebrated with great enthusiasm all over the country.

This festive day falls on the Amavasya of the month of Kartik every year exactly twenty days after Dussehra by the Hindu Calendar. This festival of lights sweets and crackers is celebrated with fun and frolic by all.

In this day, the return of Lord Rama to Ayodhya after gaining victory over Ravana is memorable. To welcome him back and to express their joy, the people of Ayodhya lighted rows of earthen lamps.

Some others believe that Goddess Lakshmi of wealth and prosperity visits every house on this night. To welcome her the lights are lit throughout the night. Jains believe that in the early morning of this day Lord Mahavir attained 'Moksha or Salvation.'

The preparations start with cleaning their houses and shops. This is the best time for the manufacturers and sellers of sweets, toys and idols of gods and goddesses, crackers, candles etc. As people are eager to purchase new clothes, utensils, greeting cards and other things, there is great hustle-bustle in every market. These market areas are decorated and they undoubtedly draw a lot of crowd.

On the day of Diwali, everyone is happy and mirthful. Clad in new clothes they visit their friends and relatives. Sweets and greetings are exchanged.

At night people worship Lord Ganesh and Goddess Lakshmi with great devotion. People decorate their houses with illuminating lamps, candles and electric bulbs.

The sight of these glittering lights is very enchanting as the night appears to be under the spell of a full moon. Children let off fireworks. All the variety of crackers like anars, rockets, lighting pencils, etc. is seen.

Fireworks must be under the supervision of elders as any folly can lead to injuries, burns and fire hazards. Many fire tenders are placed at different areas for ready help in case of need. All people young and old who take part in the happy occasion must be careful so that accidents of such harm do not occur.

Some people wrongly believe that they should gamble on the day of Diwali. Gambling is a social evil and people must keep away from this practice.

Diwali is the festival of wealth, prosperity and happiness. It is the festival celebrated by the majority of Indians in every nook and corner of the country. As such, it has become a symbol of unity in diversity.

☆☆☆

DR. MANMOHAN SINGH

Dr. Manmohan Singh is a member of the Indian National Congress party, and became the first Sikh Prime Minister of India on May 22, 2004.

He was born on 26 September 1932, in Gah, Punjab (now in Chakwal district, Pakistan). He has an Undergraduate (1952) and a Master's degree (1954) from Panjab University, Chandigarh; an Undergraduate degree (1957) from Cambridge University (St. John's College) and a PhD (1962) from Oxford University (Nuffield College).

The University of Oxford awarded him an honorary Doctor of Civil Law degree in June 2005, and in October 2006, the University of Cambridge followed with the same honour. Singh married Gursharan Kaur in 1958, and they have three daughters.

India's fourteenth Prime Minister, Dr.

Manmohan Singh is rightly acclaimed as a thinker and a scholar. Dr. Singh's academic credentials were burnished by the years he spent on the faculty of Punjab University and the prestigious Delhi School of Economics.

He had a brief stint at the UNCTAD Secretariat as well, during these years. This presaged a subsequent appointment as Secretary General of the South Commission in Geneva between 1987 and 1990.

In 1971, Dr. Singh joined the Government of India as Economic Advisor in the Commerce Ministry. This was soon followed by his appointment as Chief Economic Advisor in the Ministry of Finance in 1972.

Among the many Governmental positions that Dr. Singh has occupied are Secretary in the Ministry of Finance; Deputy Chairman of the Planning Commission; Governor of the Reserve Bank of India; Advisor of the Prime Minister; and Chairman of the University Grants Commission.

In what was to become the turning point in the

economic history of independent India, Dr. Singh spent five years between 1991 and 1996 as India's Finance Minister.

His role in ushering in a comprehensive policy of economic reforms is now recognized worldwide. In the popular view of those years in India, that period is inextricably associated with the persona of Dr. Singh.

Among the many awards and honours conferred upon Dr. Singh in his public career, the most prominent are India's second highest civilian honour, the Padma Vibhushan (1987); the Jawaharlal Nehru Birth Centenary Award of the Indian Science Congress (1995); the Asia Money Award for Finance Minister of the Year (1993 and 1994); the Euro Money Award for Finance Minister of the Year (1993), the Adam Smith Prize of the University of Cambridge (1956); and the Wright's Prize for Distinguished Performance at St. John's College in Cambridge (1955). Dr. Singh has also been honoured by a number of other associations including by the Japanese Nihon Keizai Shimbun.

Dr. Singh has represented India at many international conferences and in several international organizations. He has led Indian Delegations to the Commonwealth Heads of Government Meeting in Cyprus (1993) and to the World Conference on Human Rights in Vienna in 1993.

Singh's image is generally regarded as intellectual, honest but cautious, attentive to working class people (on whose votes he was elected), and technocratic.

Although legislative achievements have been few and the Congress-led alliance is routinely hampered by conflicts, Singh's administration has focused on reducing the fiscal deficit, providing debt-relief to poor farmers, extending social programs and advancing the pro-industry economic and tax policies that have launched the country on a major economic expansion course since 2002.

Singh has been the image of the Congress campaign to defuse religious tensions and conflicts and bolster political support from minorities like Muslims, Christians and Sikhs.

In his political career, Dr. Singh has been a Member of India's Upper House of Parliament (the Rajya Sabha) since 1991, where he was Leader of the Opposition between 1998 and 2004.

☆☆☆

EID

Eid is a Muslim term which means festival. Muslims throughout the world celebrate three Eid's during a year. Ramzan is a month of fasting. It is a very strick fast which does not allow even a sip of water during the day.

The fast is broken daily after sunset. After the month long fasting, on the day after the new moon, Ramzan Eid is celebrated. This festival is formally termed as Eid-ul-Fitr.

Bakri Eid is celebrated in the memory of Hazrat Ismail's sacrifice. This festival falls about two months and nine days after Eid-ul-Fitr.

It is for this festival that Muslims who can afford, go on pilgrimage to Mecca. This pilgrimage is known as Haj. Mutton biriani is the main dish eaten on this day. This festival is formally known as Eid-ul-zuha.

The third Eid that is celebrated with great

enthusiasm is Eid-i-milad. This day commemorates the birthday of the Holy Prophet Mohammed.

Each Eid day starts with morning prayer of the mosques and Eidgahs. People wear new clothes. After the prayers they greet each other affectionately with 'Eid Mubarak'.

They eat Kheer, biriani, sewai, sheer khorma. They offer the same delicacies to guest who visit their homes on Eid days .

☆☆☆

GOOD MANNERS

Sometimes, parents advise their children not to play with bad boys. Who are those bad boys whose company is desired to be shunned?

They are, actually just children as all other children. Only they have bad manners. In other words, they don't observe good manners or they don't know what good manners are.

Maybe, they haven't been guided properly by their parents or guardians or they are so headstrong that they haven't learnt to do any good in life nor perhaps they have any inclination to do so.

If good manners are so important, then, of course, they must be learnt and followed. Good manners sometimes overlap with good habits.

Such are rising early in the morning, brushing one's teeth, having a regular bath, putting on neat and clean clothes, polishing one's shoes daily, going to school regularly and punctually, having meals at regular times, not talking while eating, obeying and respecting teachers, parents and elders, reading good books, doing homework regularly, etc.

There is a sort of courtesy which the society expects from us. For instance, if we make frequent but proper use of such words and expressions as 'Please', 'Excuse me', 'Thank you', etc. we lose nothing. These words and expressions cost nothing. We gain a lot in the esteem of others. Others also feel happier.

We should always talk in a polite language. We should never be angry nor ever call anybody names whatever the provocation. We should be truthful and candid but not blunt.

We should not hurt anybody's sentiments. We should never be dishonest or deceitful. We should never say anything irreligious, immoral, unpatriotic, unsocial, irritating or the like.

☆☆☆

HONESTY IS THE BEST POLICY

Honesty is a rare commodity in the world today. Most people prefer the easy way out which sometimes deviates from the path of honesty, for to be completely honest means facing hardships and obstacles.

Nothing succeeds like success, and many people believe it is the "end result' that matters—not the means. Therefore, even if you acquire success, money, position and respect by being just a little out of line—it doesn't really matter much.

But remember—anything acquired by incorrect and dishonest' means will never last—what will sustain is honesty, and work done honestly.

In the world of today, honesty is regarded as a hindrance in achieving success rapidly. It may appear that the 'smooth, worker' who knows exactly how to manipulate gets ahead, while the honest not so cunning person gets left way behind—but it's like the old tale of the tortoise and the rabbit. Slow and steady and honesty—wins the race.

In the end, it's not what others judge you by that counts— it's what you judge yourself as. It's how you feel about your actions and deeds—if you are one with them and feel you have achieved your goal HONESTLY—that's all that matters.

☆☆☆

HOW I SPENT MY LAST SUMMER VACATION

Parents do not want their children to idle away their time at home. Instead, they want them to explore their hidden talents, brush up their skills and become more creative.

While most of the parents prefer their kids to join coaching for dance, music and painting classes, others want them to take up sports activities like skating, karate and swimming."

My most loving father ran from pillar to post to get me a seat for the summer camp in some hi-fi school in the mega city. He always made it a point to take me with him.

As he presented me to the principals of different schools, one after the other, I felt small as if I were an animal for sale or some saleable commodity. But I knew my kind papa was only after my long term benefit.

We got the reply big "No" everywhere since every school was allowing only the students of its own school for the summer camp for which there was so much rush everywhere.

We wondered if our own school, though quite a good one but situated in a small town, could adapt itself to the changing milieu.

At last my father met the Principal of our school and the idea clicked. In fact to our surprise Ms. Jyoti Verma, the enlightened Principal of our school had already made the arrangements for the summer camp and only the announcement regarding the same was to be made on the day my father met her. The announcement was made with enhanced excitement.

Now, let me recall the summer camp itself, held in our school campus. I need not explain that though the participation was on voluntary basis, the response was tremendous.

The students were advised to attend the camp wearing school uniform only, and they did as they had been advised to do.

In all, about 550 students participated in the

summer camp. They were divided into five groups I, II, III, IV and V. Students of Group I were taught to learn painting, music and dance for two hours daily.

Games based on mathematics, English and painting were taught to students of Group II. Group III students learnt scanning of photographs and playing games using joi sticks.

Students of Group IV were taught surfing the Internet, slide presentation on power point and the concept of making software. Group V students learnt windows XP and HTML. I was in this group.

Although different groups were taught certain basic concepts and made to participate in certain specific activities, yet there were certain common activities in which anybody and everybody could participate at the particular times and days meant for such activities.

Only one had to inform a day or so earlier, so that proper arrangements could be made for him or her alongwith others who had given their consent earlier.

Such activities included hobbies like art, vocal and instrumental music, giddha, bhangra, classical and kathakali dance, science, model making, making soft toys, casting, public speaking, etc.

There were certain activities which were done on daily basis. These included group discussion, mono-acting, histrionics, election, poetry recitation in English, Hindi and regional language, debates, declamation contests, paper reading, extempore public speaking, G.K. Quiz, etc.

For pre-primary wing students there were about two hour activities such as block printing, paper mache, collage making, puppet making, mask making, free hand painting and drawing, etc.

These little kids were also taken to the crystal clear cool water shallow swimming pool with colourful sides as reflected in the ambrosial water.

The thing which left an undying mark upon my mind was the artificial snowing on the vast floor of our now made air-tight school hall were I with my friends even skated for a while. How our worthy school Principal had arranged it for us made me wonder.

Everybody was marvelled at her resourcefulness. Neither my father nor I nor anybody in the house grudged the one thousand rupees we had to pay for the fifteen day camp. Our school, always first was first to arrange such a camp in our town.

☆☆☆

HUMAN RIGHTS

Human beings are born equal in dignity and rights. These are moral claims which are present in all human individuals by virtue of their humanity alone. These claims are formulated in what is known as human rights.

Human life and human dignity have been disregarded throughout history and continue to be mis-used even to-day.

Yet, even though laws have been made to safeguard a human being's dignity, discrimination continues to exist because of prejudice, limitations, ignorance and man's' own greed for control and power.

These rights have been needed to defend slavery, ill treatment on the grounds of sex, race, colour, descent, religion, caste, and class.

The International Bill of Human Rights was founded on10th December, 1948, when the

'Universal Declaration of Human Rights' was founded by the General Assembly as a common standard of achievement for all people and nations.

The rights are of two kinds—civil and political rights. These include, the right to life, liberty, security, freedom from torture and slavery, equality, protection, fair trial, right to marriage, freedom of thought, expression, religion.

☆☆☆

IF I WERE THE PRIME MINISTER OF INDIA

I know very well that to become the Prime Minister of India is not that easy. Since I have never taken any part in politics, nor I have any affiliations with any political party, it is almost impossible for me to become the Prime Minister of India.

Still, I think there is no harm in imaging myself to be the Prime Minister of India. If I were the Prime Minister of India, I'd do a lot of good work for the people.

I do not mean to say that others who have been the Prime Ministers of India, haven't done anything in this connection. But, I think, there is no end to doing good as doing good like everything good and truthful, is infinite.

First of all, I'd give attention to India's defence, as without being a strong country India cannot make much progress and hold her head high in the comity of nations.

Defence preparedness needs a lot of money and other resources. Unless there is a strong industrial base in a country, it cannot dream to be a powerful nation even in the matter of defence. So, I'd try to set up a base for heavy and important industry in the country.

Industrialisation on a large-scale will also boost up exports and the country will become rich. India is predominantly an agricultural country. Much of its industry depends on agriculture. It is, therefore, of paramount importance to give impetus to agriculture.

Both agricultural and industrial growth will also provide inumerable jobs and thus the problem of unemployment will be solved to a great extent.

The most baffling problems of India are the population ex-plosion, poverty, illiteracy, poor medical facilities, etc. I'll pay full attention to all these problems and bring as many reforms as possible to get rid to these problems.

I'll streamline and overhaul certain crucial systems such as taxation system, banking system, education system, childcare, etc.

Much more can be said and done in the context of the topic, but let's hope for the best as one drop of practical work is better than oceans of theoretical work. Instead of making false and rosy promises, I'll focus more on real and practical work.

☆☆☆

IF I WIN A LOTTERY

Winning a lottery is an easy way to riches. For me it shall be a dream come true for I can do almost everything I wish to do.

Who doesn't desire to be rich or be a millionaire? Like others even I dream of leading a life where I am a subject of envy and friendship. I wish I could win a bumper lottery!

It is not easy to decide what I shall do if I win a large sum of money. I shall buy a big bungalow, expensive clothes for myself and shower my relatives and friends with rich gifts. I would love to tour my favourite tourist resorts. In a way I shall spend all the amount satisfying myself and my close associates.

Wait, wait, may be I don't become so selfish. After all I have a soft heart for the poor. Now to plan the expenses, I shall open schools and colleges that will impart free education or make a big hospital that will give free treatment and special attention to the poor.

I shall work for the welfare of those who are often neglected by our cruel society. I shall donate generously to the charity trusts. I shall lead a noble life.

But it is not possible to be so humanitarian. What if money spoils me? After all, it is a matter of millions! I shall become mean and stingy. 1 shall put all the money in the bank ana get huge interests. Where will be the need for me to work? I can live on the interest.

I will not study further, as it is I hate those lengthy home assignments. I can play and play all day. My parent shout at me to study so that I can make a good career and earn well. If I save the money they will not say anything. I have the money. Don't I?

Winning a lottery is still a wish. I don't know what exactly will I do. Will I satisfy my own interests or look after others or become completely idle? No one knows what lies ahead. Neither do I. If I win a lottery and become a filthy rich person.....well what will happen is .... I AM SURE TO BECOME A MAD.

METRO RAIL IN DELHI

The word Metro is generally used for underground railways all over the world. This means of travelling is a modern transportation in human beings. Delhi has been experiencing phenomenal growth in population in the last few decades.

So, the number of vehicles has been increased to 40 lakhs, these are more than' of Mumbai, Kolkatta and Chennai.

In Delhi, million of people. The life is very hectic. Today traffic on the roads of Delhi is a mix up of cycles, scooters, cars, buses, etc. resulting road accidents, traffic jam, environmental pollution and fuel wastage.

To solved this situation the Indian Government and Delhi Government is setup a company on 3rd March, 1995 named as Delhi Metro Rail Corporation Ltd. (DMRC).

Now the Metro Railway project has been started at wide level in Delhi. The Delhi government is taking interest for the people's benefits and facilities in going place to place.

The first phase of Metro Rail Project from Shahdra to Tis Hazari has been inaugurated by Prime Minister of India, Atal Bihari Vajpayee. After six months this route has expended to Rithala. Second line started from Delhi University to Central Secretariat.

This route is almost in underground partly elevated and partly on the ground. In the first phase DMRC has 52.60 kms. route. All the underground corridors are fully air conditioned and well planned for crowd.

The experts say that Delhi Metro Railway is the advantage of Delhi people. We hope this facility will give a pollution & traffic jam free Delhi. We welcome it from the depth of our hearts to government of Delhi.

☆☆☆

MY ALBUM

Albums are a treasure house of memories. I have three albums that contain pictures taken by my parents right from the time I was born to the time I started going to school.

These photographs have helped me to get a clear picture of my past and the time I was born. To begin with there are pictures of me and my mother in the hospital.

I am hardly two days old in the first photograph of my album. There are pictures of all my relatives and my family friends in my album.

They came to visit us at the hospital and I look really small in the arms of various aunts and uncles who are seen cuddling me very lovingly.

The next section of my album includes photographs of my first birthday celebration. My birthday had been celebrated at home. There were many children who attended the party.

Even in those photograph I look quite unware of all that is going on around me. How I wish I was able to enjoy that party. The snaps show how much fun the older children had.

There was a big cake in the shape of a train and my parents held my hand while they cut the cake for me. The other highlight of my album is my head shaving ceremony.

That was the day when all the hair from my head was shaved off after a ritual performed by priests. All those have been captured in these photographs and even today my family and I relive those past moments as we glance through the album.

My album is my best friend today as it has pictures of all the friends I knew as a very little boy and those friends who have gone away.

Whenever I look at their pictures my eyes fill up with tears but I feel thankful that I had been able to click so many photographs which have always helped me remember all the good times that I have had.

☆☆☆

I take good care of my albums. These are photographs that can never be produced again since my past can never come back again.

So I show my albums to my friends who visit me today and we all go on a nostalgic journey with the past.

☆☆☆

MY AMBITION

A life without any ambition or aim is worthless. Every person has an ambition in his life. I also have an ambition. I want to become a teacher.

Teaching is the noblest profession in the world. Doctors, Engineers, Pilots, Scientists etc. are all the products of a teacher. A teacher gives direction to the life of a child. The teacher shapes the future of a nation.

I will complete my studies and do B.Ed. Then I will work in a school. I will teach in a village. I wish to teach those, who are away from education.

I want to spread education in the far off areas Of my country. It will not be a source of earning only. It will be a worship for me. I want to teach for the sake of teaching only.

I want to prepare those illiterate and poor people for future. I wish to make them aware of the progress being made by the world. I want them to become Scientists, Doctors, Engineers etc. I wish they would carry forward my dream with them.

My ambition is to educate poor farmers and their families. I want them to be familiar with new agricultural techniques. I want to make them educated enough to understand good and bad.

I want them to play a vital role in the development of our country. I can do all this by becoming a good and well learned teacher. I pray to God to help me in this task. I am sure one day I will fulfil my ambition.

☆☆☆

MY FAVOURITE BIRD

My favourite bird is the sparrow. The sparrow is a very common bird. It is to be seen anywhere and everywhere, where human beings live.

The sparrow is small in size. It has dark brown wings. The under side of its body is lighter in colour. It has small beady eyes and a small beak.

It is a busy and active bird. It wakes up early in the morning. It twitters all the time. Its cheerful twittering wakes up people from their sleep in the mornings.

Many sparrows come and sit on my window sill every morning. They twitter so loudly that it is impossible for us to continue sleeping. We have to wake up, open our balcony door and throw some grains to them. Then they hop about and merrily peck at the foodgrains.

The sparrow is a friendly bird. It likes the company of human beings. It is always to be seen close to people's houses. It makes friends very easily.

Once it knows that you will not hurt it, it hops right inside your house and flies about all over the place. If you get into the habit of feeding sparrows, they hop into your room to remind you that they are hungry.

They are quite intelligent. They notice in which container you store your foodgrains. If you are busy they will fly in and help themselves to the grain, if the container is open.

As birds are such friendly creatures, I wish more and more people would make friends with them, and be kind to them.

★★★

MY FAVOURITE LEADER

Mahatma Gandhi was the greatest man of the 20th century; he was respected by the whole world. The greatest scientists, Eienstein, said that the coming generation would not easily believe that such a man ever lived on the earth.

The greatest thing about him was that he was a human to the core and has a loving heart for the poor and the homeless. He felt for all and wished well to the entire humanity.

Mohandas Karamchand Gandhi was born in Porbandar, in the Kathiawar region of Gujarat on 2nd October, 1869. He received his early education at home. His father advised his son to go to England for higher studies. In England, Gandhiji qualified for the bar.

But on his return from England he did not succeed as a lawyer. So he went to South Africa. There he found that his countrymen were suffering under cruel laws. He led a protest movement successfully. His movement was entirely non-violent.

Returning to India in 1916, he threw himself into politics. He started the non-violent and non-cooperation movements. He was sent to Jail many times and thousands of his countrymen followed him.

A long agitation finally forced the British Government to grant independence to India on 15th August, 1947.

Subsequently it was renamed as India and Pakistan. This caused untold sufferings to life and property on both sides of the borders.

But the Father of the Nation—Bapu as he was called-was not in Delhi to rejoice. He was in distant Naokhali in East Bengal trying to bring peace among the Hindus and Muslims there.

Mahatma Gandhi lived a splendid long life. He achieved the greatest of his wishes—the freedom of India. He also wished to see India prosperous but God willed it otherwise.

Three bullets from a misguided young man finished his glorious career. He met a martyr's death, for he was pleading for Hindu-Muslim unity and this was not acceptable to certain self-interested and shortsighted people.

Mahatma Gandhi has set a standard before us. He has shown that great heights can be reached by man. By his life and later death he has served his mother country, and he has served humanity no less. He has shown the world the true way to peace.

☆☆☆

MY FIRST FLIGHT

My uncle lives in Mumbai. He is a big police officer there. Once he promised me to take me to Mumbai by air. But for long he could not fulfil his promise. It was because his duties were so strict that he could not visit us in Delhi for quite some time.

Last week, he had to come to Delhi in connection with some criminal case. He had also to go back hurriedly. But he remembered his promise and took me along with him.

As we reached the airport, soon we heard the announcement asking us to board the Boeing-21 by which we had to travel. We climbed up the stairs and entered the aeroplane. We took our seats. My uncle asked me to fasten the safety belt. I did so.

Soon, the aeroplane made a deafening sound. Its wings began to rotate. At first the rotation was slow but within a few moments it became horribly fast.

The plane began to run on the tarmac. Suddenly, it moved upwards. Quickly, it reached high up in the sky and seemed to be touching the clouds. I looked downwards through the window.

The houses seemed like small models. The men and animals looked like ants. The rivers and canals seemed to be thread-like streaks.

Within a few hours it was announced that we had reached the sky over Mumbai. Now, the aeroplane started downward movement. It was landing.

It reached the airport and began to run on the tarmac. The movement of its wings became slower and slower till finally it came to an end.

As the plane was now standing motionless on the tarmac, we came out of it as other passengers did. Our luggage was checked by the customs people and then we were allowed to go. Indeed, I can never forget this first flight by an aeroplane.

☆☆☆

ONE DAY WHEN I FELL ILL

I am very careful about my health. I take my meals regularly and exercise daily. It is rare that I fall ill. I do not like sickness but it does not care for your likes and dislikes. For me sickness means being idle and lonely. I realised it only a few days back when I fell ill.

I remember that evening when it rained heavily and together with my two friends I went outside. Despite my mother's advise not to get wet, we stayed outside talking, laughing and enjoying the cool weather. We continued to play in the rain till it was very dark and my friends had to leave.

Next day I got up unusually early. When I tried to move out of the bed I felt dizzy. My head ached and I felt restless. I pushed aside the blanket I had covered myself with, and tried to sleep again.

After some time when my mother came to wake me, as she does every morning, I did not feel like getting up. She touched my forehead and found it to be warm as I was in the grip of fever. She checked my temperature and found that the mercury thread of the thermometre was touching 101°F.

I could not go to the school. I was happy to miss my maths test as I did not study for it. My father phoned the Principal and informed him about my illness and failure to attend the classes.

A doctor was called. He prescribed some tablets and told me not to move out of the bed that day. The tablet tasted bitter and the worst was when it got stuck and dissolved in the mouth itself.

I ate my breakfast in bed. My sister brought milk and toast for me. As I was supposed to take complete rest no one stayed in my room for long. I was left alone so that I could sleep undisturbed. I felt even more restless and could not sleep.

I wished that I get well within seconds so that I can join the others. To add more to my bad state my favourite cousin came unexpectedly. He had come to invite me to join his friends. They were going on a picnic. He teased me, though lovingly, that I fell ill only to miss a great day. I could do nothing except curse my illness quite liberally.

During lunch hour I had to do with porridge while others enjoyed the usual meal. How much I envied them! They came to enquire about any improvement and for a while I felt myself important. I had begun to realise what it really meant to be sick.

Even during the evening I was confined to bed while my friends played outside. Finally I made up my mind, sickness or no sickness, there shall be no other day in bed for me.

It was porridge again for my dinner but I felt better. The medicines showed their effect and luckily my fever came down. I was happy again.

Next day I was all by myself but I had learnt a lesson. I shall take every care not to fall ill ever again and obey the elders.

☆☆☆

RAKSHA BANDHAN

Fairs and festivals hold a special value in our life. Their place is permanent. We can miss our important chores but not our festivals. Since they are the very life-breath of our religion and culture. They remind us of our splendid past.

The festival of Raksha Bandhan is the festival of pure love and brotherhood. Sisters tie sacred threads to the wrists of their brothers, thereby reminding them of their great responsibility.

The brothers pledge to defend the honour of their sisters. This bond of love and affection is very unique. A piece of thread becomes a sacred promise, never to be snapped. It is renewed every year. This bond of love takes a permanent shape.

All over India sisters—married or unmarried young or old visit their brothers. They tie the piece of thread. They offer sweets and pray for the long life of their brothers. In return, the brothers give them some token money. The idea is to exchange brother-sister love, a love which is priceless.

This festival of brother-sister love has historical back ground. It is age-old. It has been celebrated for centuries together. It is said that Rani Karmavati of Mewar sent 'Rakhi' to the Mughal Emperor Humanyun, beseeching him for her help. Humanyun acceded to the request. He helped her out of the crisis.

These days 'Rakhis' have become a roaring business. They are made at a high cost of crores of rupees. Many a shopkeeper's sole business is buying and selling of Rakhis. The bazaars are decked like a bride.

As far as the eyes can see, there are colourful and very expensive Rakhis. The other shops which have a quick business are those of sweets. People throng them. They purchase sweets worth in gold. After Diwali, Raksha Bandhan is the greatest festival of the people. It strengthens the sacred bond of love and brotherhood. It must be observed in that spirit.

SOCIAL SERVICE–TODAY

Social service has been and even today is the greatest need of India. Since Raja Ram Mohan Roy's period to the days of Mahatama Gandhi, many great men and women have devoted themselves selflessly to the cause of social service.

However the problem of social evils still persists. Thus social reform should be the religion of all the Indians. It is only then that we can recapture our ancient glory and fame. We must all unite ourselves and try to bring about social reform for the betterment of our nation.

We have to be unselfish while trying to improve the lot of our fellow beings. Let us consider a few ways by which a young educated Indian can serve his nation.

The main problem in our country is that of poverty. If we could raise funds regularly so that we can provide money for some poor people it would be a great service to them.

It may not be possible for us to fill homes of the millions of poor people in India but by sharing a little of our own money, but we could organize public functions where the rich and influential can contribute and help to build a capital that can be invested in a bank. The interest from this sum can be used by poor orphans and old people who have no homes.

We could help farmers to apply for loans and educate them about the best ways to improve their agriculture. Money is not the only kind of help we can impart.

Education and know - how can also help the farmer to approach his work with sense. He can then use modern methods to improve his farm production.

The dowry system is another evil in our country. By organizing street plays, seminars and by talking to as many people we can about the evils of this system we can help the millions of Indian women who have to undergo the humiliating experience of taking a dowry from their parents.

We have to educate our society about the evils of casteism, provincialism and communalism. We must make the society aware of the need for national integration. All this can be achieved if we all get together and work towards the realisation of an India that is rid of all these evils.

★★★

SPORTSMAN SPIRIT

Life is full of failures and success When we play a game too, we may either win or lose. "Sportsman spirit" is the spirit of accepting one's success with humility.

One of the main advantages of playing any sport is that it teaches us to cope with these failures and disappointments that come our way. After being defeated in a game repeatedly one begins to learn to fight better yet accept one's defeat better.

The same can be said to apply to one's life too. There are times when we fail at our jobs or we fail to do our duty or we may even lose some great things in life. If we lose hope and curse our fate we can never progress in our life.

There was once a man who lost all his money and property in his business. The man was practically reduced to nothing. He had a great deal of sportsman spirit and he managed to get a hold over himself in such a way that he started building his business up from scratch.

He had been defeated at the game of business by his competitors but he had been a sportsman in school and this helped him to remember the time he had been defeated by the better opponent. He recalled how the other team's calibre had in fact inspired him to match up to their level and improve himself.

Thus, it is always possible to cultivate a sportsman spirit and go through life happily. The parents and teachers of students can play an important role in inculcating some values in their children about the need to keep one's chin up even in the face of adversity.

Indoor and outdoor games can always be provided for children so that they acquire training in the game of loss and gain.

★★★

THE BHAGAVAD GITA

The Shrimad Bhagwad Geeta is an integral part of Mahabhararta, which is our third important scripture. From Mahabharata, a vital section of 700 verses spread over 18 chapters has been compiled to form Shrimad Bhagwad Geeta.

In the battlefield of Kurukshetra when Kauravas and Pandavas came face to face in armed conflict with their relatives, cousins and loved ones in opposite camps, it was natural for Arjuna to get confused and confounded.

They were his cousins and relatives, how could he slay them? Although Pandavas had been wronged, betrayed, harassed and insulted, yet Arjuna's mind witnessed an intense duel. He could not decide the right course of action for himself.

He remembered all the wrongs, deceptions and tortures of the Kauravas, yet questions like "How can I fight them?" "What should one do in such a situation?" boggled his mind. These were perplexing questions, which posed a big problem for him.

At that time Lord Krishna advised and guided Arjuna. He explained, "You are not fighting relatives; you are fighting intruders and aggressors. If one is fighting for selfish interests one should yield and leave.

But if one is fighting for common good – for the entire society, then one must destroy the unrighteous, anti social elements." When a mother kills her unrighteous son, she does it because it is just and righteous."

It was natural for Arjuna to grieve the situation he faced. People who are fighting for the cause of righteousness have to adopt the best possible means without taking into consideration their likes and dislikes of them as individuals. It is the most important principle.

Hence this was a very significant event. The message and the guidance that Lord Krishna gave to Arjuna, the spiritual wisdom imparted by him, is termed Shrimad Bhagwad Geeta. It comprises the essence of all knowledge and wisdom expounded in the Upanishads.

Bhagwad Geeta consists of the conversations between Dhritarashta and Sanjay, which contain in itself dialogues between Krishna and Arjuna. It basically talks of the larger interests of humanity and not of personal interests of the individual.

Krishna, as the speaker of the Bhagavad Gita, is referred to within as Bhagavan (the divine one). The verses themselves, using the range and style of Sanskrit meter (*chhandas*) with similes and metaphors, are written in a poetic form that is traditionally chanted; hence the title, which translates to "the Song of the Divine One".

The Bhagavad Gita is revered as sacred by Hindu traditions, and especially so by Vaishnavas (followers of Vishnu). It is commonly referred to as *The Gita*.

The content of the text is a conversation between Krishna and Arjuna taking place on the battlefield of Kurukshetra just prior to the start of the Kurukshetra war.

Responding to Arjuna's confusion and moral dilemma, Krishna explains to Arjuna his duties as a warrior and Prince and elaborates on different Yogic and Vedantic philosophies, with examples and analogies.

This has led to the Gita often being described as a concise guide to Hindu philosophy and also as a practical, self-contained guide to life.

During the discourse, Krishna reveals his identity as the Supreme Being Himself (*Bhagavan*), blessing Arjuna with an awe-inspiring glimpse of His divine universal form.

☆☆☆

THE CHANGING FACE OF A WOMAN IN INDIA

A radical change has come about since Independence, in the Indian Woman's role in society, where women automatically took a 'back seat' in all decisions which were made by the 'men' of the households and she followed blindly, never questioning, never considered important or intelligent enough to express an opinion.

The 'weaken sex' who remained a 'home commodity', whose clearly defined role involved cooking, taking care of the children, running the household on the money allotted her by her husband, being the ever patient, ever docile, ever obedient wife and mother.

Although pre-partition, women were liberated enough to step into public life, like Sarojini Naidu, Kasturba Gandhi, Bhikaji Cama, and others encouraged their peers to change the myth that women could not work outside the confines of their homes, the real radical change only came later when Indian women began to walk and work and think at par with their made counterparts.

Today, even though there is much scope for further change and advancement, women hold their own place in almost every field be it politics, teaching, the Forces, medicine, sports, legal aid, executives, entrepreneurs, engineers, bank managers, etc. What needs to alter drastically is the 'mental attitude' of people, particularly males who still dominate our society.

Unless the change comes from within, progression will be limited and a woman will not come full circle despite her endeavours and pleas, to be on equal footing as the males.

☆☆☆

THE CHILDREN'S DAY

It was the 14th November 1889 when the Great National hero Pt. Jawaharlal Nehru was born. This freedom fighter with his indomitable strength and strong determination liberated India from the clutches of the British.

During the period of the freedom struggle, he did not ignore or forget the precious wealth of the nation - children. He was greatly attached to them and would sneak a few hours to spend in their lovely company.

He was fond of them all, irrespective of any disparity. He liked to be among them, chat with them and listen to them patiently. The children obviously loved him and respected him.

He was called "Chacha Nehru" by them. Hence 14th November has an importance of its own. The 14th November is celebrated every year with enthusiasm in India. The day is called 'children's day' for obvious reasons. The great son of India is remembered by crores of children and other people.

On the occasion homages are paid to the great leader. Early in the morning on that day, people assemble in Shanti Van to pay homage to Nehru. High officials and other visitors place wreaths at the Samadhi.

Prayers and hymns are chanted. Many tributes are paid to the great leader for his magnificent achievement. He is remembered the world over on this day.

Children can be seen in a jovial mood, celebrating the occasion and singing with full gusto in praise of Nehru. They are seen in pretty dresses. They organize cultural programmes and recitation of patriotic songs.

Every school celebrates this day. They extend invitations to some leaders or V.I.P.S. They laud the children and give away prizes to the children. Sweets are distributed and speeches are delivered by the chief guests.

The commendable work of Pt. Nehru is

highlighted and children are advised to tread on the path shown by the great leader. They are advised to imbibe the values and qualities of leadership, fearlessness tenacity and sound character.

☆☆☆

THE CINEMA

Cinema is one of the most wonderful gifts of science and has created a niche for itself in the hearst of people of all ages, sections and groups. In today's fast life cinema is one of the cheapest forms of entertainment for millions of people. It is a good pastime for people.

From its beginning and till now, cinema industry has made a rapid progress. In the beginning there were black and white movies which have been replaced by coloured movies. The number and quality of cinema halls has increased manifold. New and modern techniques are being applied to get the best results.

Big cinema posters with attractive poses are seen on the walls of cities and towns for advertising and announcing the new coming movies in the city. Long queues of fans can be seen before the booking windows to get their tickets booked in advance.

Cinema is source of enjoyment and entertainment and also serves as a recreational device. It suits people of all tastes and all types. The educative value of cinema also cannot be ignored.

It is a source of knowledge and information of the happenings around us. There are religious movies which attract people in towns and villages and have a soothing effect on them. Historical cinema carries us into the past society, culture and lifestyle.

Social films expose social evils of illiteracy, dowry system, untouchability and casteism and thus leads to social reforms by awakening the public. Some films awaken the masses politically by exposing rich people and politicians who exploit and cheat the poor people.

The art films made in India have earned a good name abroad and are being appreciated by public. The cinema industry enables thousands of people to earn livelihood. It presents a great opportunity for aspiring stars, singers, writers and poets to develop their talents and earn name and fame through this industry.

But cinema has proved harmful also. Now-a-days the films are full of sex and violence which leave bad effect on the children. They learn bad habits from them and must see films whatever may come.

For this, they leave their classes and steal money from their parent's pocket. They try to copy film stars in fashion and speech and learn to smoke and drink and thus waste their parent's hard-earned money.

☆☆☆

THE EVIL OF PRICE-RISE

Everyday the rise in prices of all necessities of life is very harmful. The poor are hard hit. They can not make both ends' meet respectably. They live from hand to mouth. They have very meagre (little) to spend.

Time and again we see the price index takes an upward long jump. The prices of all house hold articles have begun to touch the sky. It disturbs the family budget very badly.

The middle-class people who are mostly salaried class, face great sufferings. Their sorrows are endless. They keep up their face by borrowing or seeking hand loans. Their position is extremely tight.

The frequent price rise affects the purchasing power. Money loses its face value. It is no more a standard money. The value of Indian rupee in the International money market has fallen down abruptly. Even a heavy pay packet of 'thousands' fail to purchase a bag full of articles.

One has to put a brake on his wants and needs which are ever-increasing. They say do not delimit your needs but increase your means of income so as to cope with the rising prices.

The things are becoming dearer day by day. They are becoming beyond the approach of the common man. He looks at them with wishful eyes. The cooking gas, petrol, edibles, corn and cloth are becoming costlier everyday. The Government should rise to the occasion.

It must check this inordinate (excessive) rise in prices. The situation is growing very alarming. It is greatly grim and gruesome. There is little hope of its salvage (relief). Let the government take drastic steps to control it. It must curtail its wasteful expenditure.

Too much tours and jaunts by the politicians and ministers to the foreign countries must be stopped at once. Let us be austere. 'Simple living and high thinking' should be our national motto. Simplicity is the only alternative against these sky rocketing prices.

THE IMPORTANCE OF BOOKS

Books are a storehouse of knowledge. All that men have observed, learnt and experienced over the centuries has been enshrined in books. In other words, it is in books that the great minds of the past ages are kept safe for generations to come.

Books are our best friends. Even our closest friends and nearest relatives may part company with us in time of adversity, but books always stand by us. They stand by us through thick and thin. They never betray us.

When the dark clouds of misery engulf us from all sides and we feel helpless, books come to our rescue. We read them, consult them and regain hope and confidence which no living human being could impart

In earliest times, man was uncivilized and barbarian. Someone thought of writing and when he joined the written pages to form a unit, the first book took its birth.

Previously, books were handwritten and were sometimes lost As the printing press came, books began to be printed in thousands such that if one book or some books were lost there were almost always a few more left to keep the author's ideas alive.

Now, we have books of all kinds on all branches of life. We have books on literature, philosophy, sports, history, astronomy, astrology, poetry, cookery, doll-making, soap making, physiology, hygiene, geography, mathematics, fiction, science & technology, painting, photography, drama, indeed, on any and every conceivable subject. Much depends on our own aptitude and necessity which type of books we want to read.

In the modern computer age, some people fear that the device like the internet may spell the end of books. But, as we have seen, it is a fallacy as books have their own place in our life. They are indeed, indispensable and that is an indisputable fact.

THE IMPORTANCE OF SPORTS

A person who plays a game seldom is not said to be a sportsman. A sportsman does regular practice and that punctually.

A sportsman is always possessed with the spirit of doing something wonderful and unbelieveable in his field. He does not like to be corrupted or to corrupt anybody. It is because of this performance that he is acclaimed which he has to prove in the ground where many hundreds of people watch him. So, transparency is one such quality which always lives with him.

The qualities imbibed in the field of sports in youth stand a person in good stead all his life. The first and foremost quality is the sportsman spirit.

This quality persuades a man to remain cheerful even when he loses a match. It means that one should play a game for the sake of game and not just for victory.

Life is also a field where one acts. It is one's choice to accept it as a happy field full of sports or joys or a valley of misery. One who knows the art of happiness takes life as a game of sports where one is expected to play honestly and with complete sincerity to the best of his knowledge, skill and capability.

Sports help us in developing our personality. It is a pity that much attention is not paid to sports in our country. Most of the funds-are wasted on trivial items not connected with sports such as dinners, tea parties, honouring some personages from outside the realm of the sports, etc.

Our players do not even get sufficient diet. Infrastructure for sports in our country is lacking. Then there is so much bungling in the matter of selection of teams.

It is no surprise that we are not able to get a single medal in the Olympics when we shamefully realize that we are a country of one billion, or we comprise one seventh of the total population of the world.

Certainly, something must be done to overcome

this malaise at the highest level. Just the creation of a ministry of sports at the union level is not enough.

In April 2000, there was a sort of upheaval in the world of cricket when the revealations regarding match-fixing became a part of the public debate. Every lover of cricket was appalled.

As a result of all this turmoil, many voices were heard demanding banning or abandoning of the game of cricket altogether. Let us hope this is hot going to be done.

Instead, we should hope that the detractors, if any, are going to be suitably punished to ensure a fair game so that it can continue providing entertainment and inspiration to millions of spectators and T.V. viewers the world over.

☆☆☆

THE IMPORTANCE OF NEWSPAPERS

The two most important things in this world are the computer and the newspaper. The newspapers give news, views, reviews and previews. Sometime the word NEWS is interpreted as North, East, West and South.

It means that the newspapers provide us information and news regarding different subjects from all the directions.

The newspapers do not give just news to us. They also give us articles on all kinds of topics such as political, social, economic, monetary, business, commerce, sports, education, health, etc.

The newspapers have different columns devoted to different topics. In them we have matrimonial, editorial, readers, employment, women's, children's and other columns.

The burning problems of the day are discussed in the newspapers. Elaborate articles by experts and specialists appear in them.

Then the readers' views and opinions are published in the Readers' Column which is also known as Letters to the Editor.

The newspapers are a very potent vehicle. They carry pow. erful advertisements which attract the attention of customers. They can make or mar a government.

That is why the press is known as the Fourth Estate after the Legistature, the Judiciary and the Executive.

The newspapers also contain book-reviews of literary, historical and other books by the scholars.

Now, the newspapers are mostly in four colours. They also have weekly columns on plants, cookery, gardening, fashions, beauty concept, etc.

We must not be misled by the views expressed in newspapers. We must weigh them on the scale of reason, as some newspapers may be prejudiced. But normally newspapers are important means for spreading literacy, health-care, etc.

☆☆☆

THE IMPORTANCE OF WORK

The very shape of human body tells us that it has been made for work. This is very evident to us if we have a look at a buffalo.

So, even nature has made human body in such a way that man is expected to make himself busy in various types of activities. Our feet and legs tell to walk and run, if possible.

The hands and arms urge us to do one or the other physical work or to carry out some kind of art activity. Over and above this, man is endowed with brain which means that we should be intelligent, wise and judicious.

Besides, man has certain qualities, both virtues and vices hidden in the heart. Nature or God perhaps don't tell us to be vicious.

That is our own choice. Nature has given us emotions and impulses and the power to think, to will, to love, to behave decently and to do good to others.

It is said that "Work is worship". It is also said, "An idle man's brain is the devil's workshop". These together mean that man must keep his limbs and mind busy which can bring him material and financial gains as well as real happiness which arises from doing useful work.

Broadly speaking, work can be of two types, that is, work for some selfish purpose or for some financial gain for oneself or for the members of one's family.

Thus when we pursue any profession or do any business, the spirit of earning is strong in us. We may sometimes have to imitate or emulate or compete to steal a march over others or not let others overtake us or outdo us.

This is altogether not an unhealthy spirit but could be good for the health and growth of society. But what is the use of underhand methods arising out of cunningness, cheating, flattery, back-biting or unhealthy short-cuts.

There are several unhealthy and undesirable professions taking their roots due to human greediness and excessive love for money and luxury which should be avoided.

It means that contentment is not a negation of work. Similarly, working too much at the cost of one's health is also bad.

It is essential that there should be a healthy balance between work and leisure and one should feel satisfied and contented with one's work even while working hard for livelihood. Getting rich by working beyond one's capacity or through wrong methods is not desirable.

The best kind of work is, however, that which is done without any selfish motive. To this category, we have social work or helping a poor relative, a friend or a stranger.

Now-a-days, even social work has become materialistic as it has become a means for earning money and several institutions offer special courses and degrees in this respect.

That is not bad. But the most important factor in doing a work is the intentions with which we do it. If our intentions are good, the work is good and valuable. Otherwise, bad intentions mar the value of even a good work.

THE JOY OF AN AIR TRAVEL

Travelling by air is one of the most exciting ways of travelling, and the Airport from where air travel begins is a place bustling with activities, people coming and going, and announcements being made to remind passengers that their flight is about to take off.

After arriving at the Airport, it is customary to deposit your baggage at the airline counter. The officer on duty examines your air ticket. Expect a queue at the counter, but wait your turn patiently—it will come.

After your tickets have been checked, the baggage is weighed. The standard baggage permitted is 20 kgs per passenger traveller on the economy class, and 30 kgs for those travelling in the first class, on both domestic and international flights.

The baggage that is not required on the flight is checked in. Normally a small bag is allowed into the aircraft, no large baggage is permitted. This is placed on the rack above your seat.

The rest of the baggage that is checked in, is kept in the storage compartment of the aircraft and delivered on arrival at the destination.

Usually, stickers and baggage tags are provided by the airlines for fixing on to the baggage. Excess baggage should always be avoided. After checking both tickets and baggage the counterfoil is returned by the airline staff with a boarding pass.

In the case of an international flight, there is a customs, immigration, and security check before the passenger actually proceeds towards the aircraft.

Now-a-days, in order to protect passengers and the aircrafts from hijackers and terrorists, strict security and restrictions have been placed. These measures have been enforced after several cases of hijacking which have left passengers very insecure and scared.

Areas where people coming to 'see off' their friends or relatives, have now been closed, as a security safeguard.

If your seat is near the window, you can look out and see the clouds so close you can almost touch them. As you ascend higher and higher, the city you just left behind looks miniature, like a doll's playground with gardens and trees.

For these few moments, it's easy to visualise what birds feel like in the sky with nothing but the clouds, your flying in space', away from the hindrance of city life.

☆☆☆

THE PEN IS MIGHTIER THAN A SWORD

The pen is mightier than a sword, is a very practical saying. What a pen can do cannot be done by a sword. The might possessed by a pen cannot be attained by a sword. Sword only knows to cut but pen can cut as well as unite.

Although, a pen looks a small object, yet it can do wonders. What actions cannot do, can be done by words. So what ever a pen writes, makes permanent imprint. We can air our ideas, we can experts our opinions and we can show our dissent with a pen.

Words can bring revolutions in the world. We have seen it that after reading the revolutionary ideas of Bhagat Singh, the youth of India threw away the British Government. Pen can bring resolutions. Many peace pacts had been signed with a pen.

The daily newspapers carry the ideas and opinions of the public in its columns. People express their opinions regarding the happenings in their countries and abroad.

They write their views regarding the policies of the government. The Government come to know about the shortcomings and positive points of their policies. Governance becomes easy.

Pen can bring communities and countries close. It can throw them apart also. Communal feelings can be inflamed by the writes to cause communal violence. On the other hand articles about unity and integrity of communities can bring them close.

Pen brings the world wide scene to us. Happenings in world can be given any shape or face by the pen. Personalities are built and ruined by the pen. Views can be distorted and misinterpreted by the pen. Such is the might of a pen.

The pen has given us a big treasure of books and epics. It brings to us the ideas of great philosophers, poets, and great thinkers of the by gone era.

Pen has its dark side also. It depends on us how to use it. It's power should be used in a positive way. It can spread the light of knowledge and peace all over the world, which a sword cannot do.

☆☆☆

THE RAMAYANA

Ramayana is a famous epic. It deals with the life of Lord Rama and was written by Valmiki in Sanskrit. It was later written in Hindi by Tulsi Das and the work is known as 'Ram Charitramanas'. Dasharatha, the king of Ayodhya had three queens and four sons. Ram was his eldest son. He was very obedient and brave.

As he was an obedient son, he left for fourteen years of exile to keep his father's words. His brother Lakshman and wife Sita also went along with him. King Dasharatha could not bear the separation and died.

Bharat, Rama's younger brother, went to the forest to bring back his brothers and sister-in-law but Rama refused to return. In the forest, they had to face many hardships. But they were always calm and peaceful. They helped many saints from demons.

Once Sarupanaka, sister of Ravan, who was a brave king of Lanka, fell in love with Lakshman and insisted on marrying him. Lakshman, a hot tempered man, cul off her nose. This made her very angry and she asked his brother Ravan to take revenge. Ravan disguised himself as a sanyasi and kidnapped Sita.

Shri Rama, with the help of Sugriv, attacked Lanka. Hanumanji played a very important role in finding Sita. Ravan, along with his brother Kumbhkaran and son Meghnath, was killed in the battle field. Vibhishan, Ravan's brother, became the king of Lanka.

From the very beginning, he was on the side of Lord Rama. Sita was rescued. After completing fourteen years of exile, Rama returned to Ayodhya.

People rejoiced and welcomed them by celebrating and lighting up the city. Even today this famous festival is celebrated as Diwali. Ramayana is life history of Lord Rama. It teaches us how one should behave in society. It is a sacred book of Hindus. This book is read on all important occasions in the Hindu society.

THE SPRING SEASON

Here in India we have all the seasons of the year. Summer is followed by autumn and winter. After the end of the chilly winter, the season changes. Then comes in the spring season.

It is called the king of seasons. It ushers in cool breezes, flowers, roses and green leaves. The whole atmosphere is full of sweet smell and fragrance. One becomes young and buoyant (light-hearted).

We can call it as the Season of flowers. The buds bloom into colourful blossoms. There is a riot of colours every where. The plants sprout into big trees.

The seeds germinate into rich golden harvest. The birds sing and chirp day and night. New leaves come up. A cool breeze blows. The spring season is in full swing. Nature is at its best. In India we have all the six seasons. Their circle is incessant and endless. They come turn by turn.

But the beauty and allurement of the spring season is immense.

It is matchless. The season begins round about 15th of March every year. Then the weather is very mild and moderate. All the trees and plants shed their old leaves and shoots.

They put on fresh leaves. They look as if singing and dancing. They welcome the advent of the Season of Flowers. All sorts of plants sprout. There is plenty and prosperity every where. Greenery meets the eyes. It looks very pleasant. Parks and gardens are the most frequented places. Even the peocock dances with joy.

In the rural India, this season of flowers has a special significance. There countless fairs are held. Young girls swing (sway in rope-made swing) throughout the day in the nearest garden. They sing songs in honour of the' king of the seasons.

In our Literature, the description of the 'Spring Season' is very amazing. Many beautiful poems have been composed. The season is a symbol of youth and cheerfulness. It gives the message of undying love and merriment.

THE STUDENT & THE DISCIPLINE

In the life of a student, the value of discipline is great. His is a disciplined life, a life of self-control. He knows the value of 'First deserve then desire, first obey and then be obeyed.'

The life of a student is a life of dedication, devotion and penance. He has to observe self-control and discipline. He has to shun way wardness.

He has to be strong and firm. He has to for sake the comforts of an easy life. A student should get up early in the morning. He should leave aside laziness. He should be active and smart. He should be wide awake.

He must not shirk hard work. His diligence and labour will pay him in the long run. If he leads a dedicated life in the early period of his life, his future is bright. He will reach the heights of greatness. Success will crown him.

It is discipline which will inculcate in him good habits. It will give him the strength of character. He will develop powers of head and heart. His moral teachings and bookish knowledge should begun side by side.

Then he will come out as a pure gem. Then he is well-cut, moulded and polished. His glean will shine in every direction. He will be a model to others.

What is teaching ? It is the sum total of a few good habits. They are truth, punctuality, regularity, discipline and diligence. A student who picks up these ideal things at the earliest, remains 'the best' throughout life. He faces no hardship in later life. He tops the list in every field.

Class room and play ground are 'the nursery'of these finer traits. There they can be learnt best. Such a disciplined chap will create order out of chaos. He will set 'standard' in every walk of life. He will be 'honoured' every where.

The people around will look at him with

respectful awe. In the society he will hold a place of great pride. Respect begets respect. Similarly discipline begets discipline.

The period of school life is the best period. It is the period of learning and inculcating. It is the period of formation. Let us pick and choose good habits as many as we can.

☆☆☆

THE VISIT TO A VAISHNO DEVI

Last month we went to Vaishno Devi temple. It is situated in Jammu and Kashmir. It is one of the most famous temples of the Hindus.

I along with my family went there. We reached Jammu by train. From Jammu Bus Stand we went to Katra by bus. There is a frequent bus service from Jammu to Katra. There was a big rush of devotees at Katra. People were buying prasad at shops.

We hired a room. We rested there for some time. We took our food at a shop. From that shop we bought sticks and fleet shoes. We also bought prasad. We started our journey to Vaishno Devi temple from Katra.

It is a long journey on foot. Mostly people go to temple on foot. Others hire mules. We decided to walk. We started walking in the evening. It was very pleasant.

A large number of devotees were walking. Many people were coming back. Every body was greeting each other by saying Jai Mata Di.

It was a tough journey. It was tiring to walk on mountains. We kept on taking rest in between shelters are built along the way People stop there for sometime and take rest.

We reached Ardhkuari by the night. We passed through the cave of Garbhjune. There we took some snakes and tea and started our journey again. People were passing by, and chanting Jai Mata Di.

Some people were carrying drums with them. They were dancing on the beat of drums. It was getting cold. We reached Vaishno Devi temple early in the morning.

After reaching near the temple, we hired a room. We took our bath. We wore new clothes. We started for the temple. There was a long line of devotees. They were waiting for their turn to go in the temple.

Everybody was chanting Jai Mata Di. After an hour we entered the main temple. We had to go through a cave and offered our prayers to Vaisho Mata. Coconut is offered as prasad.

We came out of the cave. It was very peaceful and calm inside the cave. We all were feeling very happy. After taking our breakfast, we started back for Katra. It was very tiring journey, but full of solace and peace. I wish to go to Vaishno Devi every years.

☆☆☆

UNEMPLOYMENT

One of the most thought-provoking ills of our society is the problem of unemployment that millions of people in our country face today.

Highly, qualified professionals find “No vacancy” signs everywhere they go and the irony of fate is that a number of jobs come with the tag of knowing some ‘high up’ who have pulled ‘strings’ and got someone else the job, while the deserving candidate who has no ‘godfather’ waits and waits to get a break.

These are some harsh realities people face as they struggle to make ends meet. Through frustrations and financial constraints other problems manifest as well, such as violence in the form of pickpocketing, cheating, dacoity, thefts, terrorism, indiscipline, drug trafficking, smuggling and sex crimes.

The disparity between the rich and the down trodden is immense, it is but natural that the ones at the receiving end revolt!

India cannot be a strong economy unless this problem is tackled. The vast numbers bordering on the poverty line, should get adequate job opportunities. Greater stress should be laid on vocational studies—creative careers should be encouraged.

Our education system should become flexible, less rigid and result oriented. Cottage and small industries should have greater potential.

☆☆☆

WATER AND PEOPLE

The problem in India is that land features change every few kilometres and, therefore, there can be no uniform or standing national water policy which can be put into practice properly unless it takes into account the elaborate terrestrial conditions of the terrain in its diversity which is too large and whopping.

Then we have local variation depending on soil, crops sown and the mode of irrigation. The result is that whereas there may be an acute paucity of water in one area another one, not quite far away, may be suffering from the acute problem of water logging.

In certain states, as during the Green Revolution in Punjab, the underground water has been tapped to criminal excess, thus lowering the level to an alarming extent.

This local variation can be gauged from the situation prevailing in Punjab and Haryana. In

Punjab, whereas in several areas there is scarcity of water, in the districts of Ferozepur and Bhatinda there is the problem of water-logging and water there is brackish and unfit for human consumption.

In Haryana most of southern and central districts have light, loamy soils. Such soils have a higher capacity for water retention. The result is rising water tables, poor drainage, water-logging and high soil salinity.

The reverse is the case in the northern districts. In these districts, the soil is heavier. Such a soil cannot retain water for long. The result is falling water tables and soil-compacting.

There are certain steps which can easily be taken. For example — Roof top water can be tapped during the rainy season. The Union Minister for Urban Development, indicated sometime back that the roof-top water harvesting would be incorporated in building by-laws.

It is reported that the Human Settlement Technology for the conservation of rainwater has been finalised by the Indian Institute of Technology.

The farmers may be asked to change the cropping pattern by giving more emphasis on crops like sunflower which require less water.

Many of the tube-wells in certain areas are built in wells which lie at the field level. During the rainy season, often much of the water just goes down the drain.

The farmers build temporary walls around the tube-wells to prevent the water from flooding the wells which are sometimes covered. The farmers can be asked to keep the wells uncovered and unwalled during the rainy season to let the rain water flow freely into their wells. This can raise the water table of ground water to some extent.

Sometime back, it was suggested by a retired chief engineer from a state that deep bores at certain places should be made into the soil during the rainy season to let the freely-flowing rain water seep into the soil.

In areas where water-logging is a problem, channcls should bc built to carry water to the areas of scarcity. Such channels should preferably be covered to 'prevent the water from evaporating.

☆☆☆

WHEN I LOST MY DOG

Last Sunday I experienced one of the worst incidents in my life. My dog Tiger and I had gone for a walk to the garden in the morning.

It was a bright sunny day and the garden was full of joggers and old people who are regular sights at the garden.

There were children who were busy playing various outdoor games and some loners were sitting under trees or close to the tombs and meditating.

Tiger and I decided to race each other in the garden. We set a point and started running. I was so busy trying to reach the "finish" point that I lost sight of Tiger who did not quite comprehend where he had to go.

He suddenly disappeared behind a bush. I rushed to the spot where I last saw him but to my despair I could not find him anywhere behind the bush.

I ran all around the place looking behind trees and in the bushes but I couldn't spot Tiger anywhere. There were a few boys in the garden who were playing cricket.

They saw my state of panic and asked me what the problem was when I told them that I had lost my doy, they were extremely sympathetic and immediately came to my assistance.

They formed groups and we sent out a search party to locate Tiger. We looked in the tombs, we searched practically every patch of land but to no avail.

Finally I lost hope and was absolutely dejected. I decided to go home and lodge a complaint with the police and seek their help. My heart was heavy and my eyes filled with tears.

Soon they started rolling down my face and I kept wondering what Tiger's fate might be. As I approached my house I saw a familiar figure huddled under the car which was parked outside the house.

I looked carefully and to my delight and relief I found that it was Tiger who had lost his way but had been clever enough to trace his way back home. Tiger licked my face and hands and we both went back into the house feeling happy once again.

☆☆☆

WOMEN AND EDUCATION

What a change in women's status from the Vedic age to the present day? Looking back at history, we find that women were treated with respect in the Indian society.

In the Vedic age women were educated. However, as society became orthodox, there was change in their status.

They were confined to the four walls of kitchen and occupied in rearing children. Men became bread winners and it was considered necessary for them to be educated. The roles of men and women was thus seperated.

But now the social scene has considerably changed. Women all over the world are being educated in almost every field that men were so far normally associated with.

The knowledge of arts, science, technology and politics is no longer the privilege of men alone. Women have begun to study these subjects and have brought great credit to themselves and their nation by contributing actively in those fields.

As a result every school is now conscious of imparting education to girls. Some states even give incentive to them.

This has been done primarily because even today there are some orthodox people who feel that a woman's place is only in her home. Yet one cannot deny the fact that it is absolutely essential to educate the women in any society.

If the woman is an educated mother, she can bring up children much better. Being aware of the events and thoughts prevailing in the world, she can help to broaden the horizon for her children.

In case the male in the family is unable to work for some reason, the woman can be financially independent too. She can supplement the income of the family by taking up a job, thus providing a better standard of living for her children and husband.

Wisdom requires that girls should be sent to school and later to college and encouraged to lead the society. It has been said that "You educate a man and you educate one person, but when you educate a woman you educate a whole family".

The influence of a woman in the home is greater than man and her education spreads within the family. Her education is most important because she is the first teacher of her child and is it not true that the hand that rocks the cradle rules the world".

☆☆☆

WOMEN IN INDIA

Since independence there has been much improvement in the lot of women in India. The women of India who form 50% of the population have equal opportunities and rights and can aspire for any position and status in the society.

Many of them are in top positions in various fields of life. A few of them have been great and big political leaders, entrepreneurs, administrators and business persons.

This marked change in their outlook, social and economic status reflect the fact that their emancipation has been almost complete. It is a fact that Indian women have much better status than their counterparts in many other developing countries.

Today women in India are well conscious of their rights and privileges and they are politiacally, socially, economically and educationally no more backward. Their participation in democratic process and elections has been quite impressive. In a large number of constituencies women voters outmember men voters on the days of polling.

They are contesting elections on various levels in far greater members. Their political wisdom and social sagacity has now been fully recognized. The status of women in India in modern times has undergone a sea change.

During the last few decades India has produced many great women leaders, social workers, administrators, reformers and literary personalities like Mrs. Annie Besant, Mrs. Vijaya Lakshmi Pandit, Mrs. Sucheta Kripalani, Mrs. Indira Gandhi, Raj Kumar Amrit Kaur, Padmaja Naidu, Mother Teresa, Mahadevi Verma, Subhadra Kumari Chauhan, Amrita Pritam etc. India really feels very proud because of these great women and their great achievements in various fields of our life.

Their contribution in the fields of art, science sports etc. has also been equally significant and memorable. Their active participation in our various social, political, economical, educational, scientific and other nation-building activities as mothers, wives, sisters and daughters has been of vital importance in taking the country to greater heights of achievements and fulfillment. And yet there is no room for any complacency.

A working woman helps her husband by bringing additional income, but as a housewife she has no help from her husband. Men regard household chores below their dignity and so never help women in their household-work. Thus, women are doubly burdened, which often causes tension, maladjustment and family problems.

There is much to be done towards emancipation of women in India. They are still subdued and dominated by men and cannot assert their equality as desired in every walk of life. In a number of our states there still exists child marriage, but widow marriages are not allowed. Girls are still given away in marriages against their will.

Then there is dowry system. Poor parents

cannot afford to give dowry and so are obliged either to keep their daughters unmarried or give them away in marriages to unmatched husbands. In spite of equal status of women granted by our law, the women are discriminated against.

The vast gap between theory and practice is too obvious not to be noticed. Women, specially in rural India, still find themselves weak, helpless and exploited. The rate of literacy among them is quite low. Sometimes they are treated no better than commodities.

They are still confined to the four walls of a house engaged in the household drudgery. They have been forced by arrogant men to play a totally subordinate role because they are economically and socially not self-dependent.

This has been further helped by our old, outdated and conservative customs. Their hard work and toil as housewives and working-women, though significant enough to run a household and family, still go unrewarded and unrecognised.

The present status of women in India has to be

further consolidated and improved. It cannot be achieved unless women themselves come forward and organize themselves as a power to be reckoned with. They should stop thinking in terms of weaker sex.

They should rise as one powerful body and fight the menace of dowry and child-marriage. They should fight tooth and nail wherever there is their abuse, exploitation, humiliation and injustice. They should raise their voice in unity against all social evils and male arrogance. They should wage a relentless war against "apartheid of sex".

Indian women are intelligent, hard-working, courageous and full of love, pity, and compassion. With all these qualities of head and heart they are quite competent in shattering all the bondages that bound them in traditional subordination and slavery.

Endowed with the qualities of beauty, love, strength, tolerance, sacrifice, creativity etc. they can do wonders for themselves and for others.

In the present day Indian world they can further

consolidate their position and redefine their relationship with men based on equality and mutual respect by using their strengths more wisely. It is of no use to curse and bemoan their fate as weaker sex and housewives.

They should unite and struggle against injustice, discrimination, illtreatment, abuse and exploitation. Much really depends on women themselves. The future of women in India seems bright but it is women themselves who can ensure it by being vigilant alert and united.

They will have to raise their voice against any violation of their rights and privileges. It is said that God helps those who help themselves and it is equally true in case of the equality and liberty of women in India.

☆☆☆

LETTERS

TO FRIEND INVITING HIM TO A HILL STATION.

41, Shimla
12th May 2007
My dear Ajay

I reached Shimla yesterday. I was tired of the scorching heat of the plains. I'm glad to state that Shimla is just like a paradise. It is rightly called like Mussourie, the Quean of Hills. It is all pleasant here.

A cool breeze is always blowing. The rain is frequent but it is not inundating as in the plains. All around Shimla there are lush green forests of pine and other trees. There are sparkling springs everywhere.

I, therefore, invite you to come here and stay

with me during the summer vacation. Then we'll visit Jakhu, Kufri and other places and have frequent walking trips in forests and over the hills. I live here with my uncle who is a very generous, jolly person.

Convey my regards to your revered parents.

Yours sincerely

Sachin Sharma

TO FRIEND SYMPATHISING ON HER/ HIS FAILURE IN THE EXAMINATION.

15, Rama Vihar
New Delhi.
4th April, 2008

My dear Shubham

Just now I have learnt that you have failed in your examination. I am really shocked to know all this. I did not believe my ears. You were a sincere student. You had been burning mid night oil. You could not fail. This is injustice. There is something wrong somewhere.

Your failure may be due to your accident. You had to remain in the hospital for a month. Dear friend, take heart. Do not feel disappointed. After all our failures are our stepping stones to success. Work hard once again. This time you will succeed. You will top the class.

With sympathy,
Yours Sincerely
Rahul Bajaj

WRITE A LETTER TO YOUR FRIEND CONGRATULATING HIM ON WINNING A SCHOLARSHIP.

11/5, Bali Nagar
New Delhi
4th March, 2008

My dear Deepak

My joy knew no bounds to learn that you have won a scholarship in the Secondary Examination. Please accept my heartiest congratulations on your brilliant success.

It is good you have maintained your family tradition. You are in no way less intelligent than your elder brother and sister. You have brought a distinction to your school. I am very proud of having an intelligent friend like you.

Please convey my heartiest congratulations to your parents.

Yours sincerely

Rahul

LETTER TO YOUR FRIEND CONGRATULATING HIM ON HIS HAPPY WEDDING.

5/62, Karol Bagh
New Delhi
My dear Vijay

Let me congratulate you most heartily upon your wedding, which marks the beginning of a new chapter in your life's career and wish you both all success and prosperity. Let every new year unite your hearts in loving affection more and more closely and bring you tidings of happiness.

May heaven bless you both with long life, health and wealth is the earnest prayer of.

Your loving friend

Hitesh Sharma

LETTER OF APOLOGY TO YOUR FRIEND

15/25, Mayur Vihar
New Delhi.
4th April, 2008

Dear Geeta

Are you still angry with me? You have not replied to my earlier letter. I miss your company and sincerely wish for the good times to return.

I know I have done wrong by suspecting you of selfishness. It all happened due to Shivani who is jealous of our friendship and poisoned my ears when you could not come to the Party. I feel sorry that I shouted at you even without giving you a chance to explain.

I offer my sincere apology and extend my hand of true and close friendship. Let us be fast friends once again. I hope you will come to my house very soon. With love to you,

Yours sincerely

Sarita Verma

REPLY TO THE ABOVE LETTER

4/21, Naya Bazar
Faridabad
20th April, 2008

Sarita Verma

Sorry for not replying earlier. The reason was that my younger brother was hospitalised for three days due to serious dehydration. Now he is back at home and recovering.

There is no reason why I should be angry with you. I have known Padma for a long time and when you behaved the way you did I knew that Padma had played the trick.

I have no grudge against you. I shall always remain your fast friend. I shall visit you very soon. There is so much to talk about. Just wait till we-meet.

With love
Yours sincerely
Geeta Aggarwal

TO PRINCIPAL FOR FEE CONCESSION.

16th April, 2008.

To

The Principal

Golden Public School

Faridabad

Sir

I am a brilliant student of your school. I always stand first in my class. I'm also good at sports and extra-curricular activities.

However, my father is a very poor man He is a peon in a private firm. His salary is very low. He is unable to pay my school fees.

I'll, therefore, be grateful if you grant me full fee concession.

Thanking you.

Yours obediently

Joyti Kukreja

Class 9th

Roll No.15

TO THE PRINCIPAL FOR CONDONATION OF SHORTAGE OF LECTURES.

15th February, 2008.

To

The Principal

DPS Public School

Faridabad

Sir

During the last two months I had to get leave from school frequently. It was because my mother was in hospital on account of serious kidney trouble. Thank God, she has recovered now. However, my lectures have gone short by ten per cent.

I shall be grateful if you condone the shortage of my lectures. I assure you that I'll try my best not to miss a single lecture from now till date of the examination.

Yours obediently

Tanvir Dutt

Class - X A

TO THE PRINCIPAL FOR BRINGING ABOUT SOME IMPROVEMENT IN THE WORKING OF SCHOOL LIBRARY AND CANTEEN.

18th February, 2008.

To

The Principal

Akash Ganga International Public School

Faridabad

Sir

Our school library is one of the best in the Faridabad. But its working can be improved further if it is shifted from the ground floor to the first floor. Thus it will get an exclusive situation and the effect of noise and pollution on readers will be minimised.

Similarly, if the canteen is shifted from its present situation to the block behind the cycle-scooter-shed, its smoke and smells will not spread in the school campus.

Yours obediently

Priyanka Aggarwal

Roll No. 16

Class - X A

APPLICATION FOR THE POSITION OF COMPUTER TEACHER.

25, Ansari Road, Daryaganj
New Delhi
30th April, 2008.
To
The Principal
Jain Happy School
Gole Market
New Delhi
Respected Sir/Madam

With reference to your advertisement dated 25th April, 2008, in the Hindustan Times, I hereby apply for the position of Computer Teacher.

As regards my academic and other qualifications, I want to say that I passed both my BCA and MCA exmainations from the Delhi University in the year 2002 and 2006 respectively. Thereafter, I also attended a fortnight one year Diploma Computer Application Course at Delhi, IICE Institute in 1999.

My date of birth is 27th July, 1978, I passed

both Matriculation and Senior Secondary examinations from the DAV Public School, Delhi Board in 1996 and 1998 respectively and was placed in the first division in both.

At present I'm working as a Computer Assistant in a Computer Lab of moderate standing. I'm drawing a meagre Rs. 6500/- per month which is quite incommensurate with my qualifications. I'm writing as I expect better emoluments in your institution.

I need not stress that I can operate computer well and put it to various uses such as typing, designing, etc. in a perfect way.

If appointed, I promise to work diligently and bring laurels to your institution through my spirit of devotion and dedication.

Yours faithfully

Rakesh Sharma

LETTER TO YOUR FATHER THANKING HIM FOR A GIFT ON YOUR BIRTHDAY.

Ramjas Hostel No. 4
Ramjas Public School
Anand Parbat
New Delhi.

2nd May, 2008.

My dear father

My friends celebrated my 15th birthday with great rejoicing. I was heaped with gifts and presents. But the present sent by you and mumma was matchless in beauty and utility.

I thank you from the core of my heart for the pretty gift. It gave me great pleasure to receive your lovely gift. It is a very beautiful camera. I will cherish it as a token of your love for me. The camera is very good and all the friends of my hostel have appreciated the gesture. This shows your deep affection for me.

Kindly pay my regards to mumma and Ritu.
Yours' lovingly

Pramood Kumar

LETTER TO FATHER REQUESTING HIM TO INCREASE YOUR MONTHLY ALLOWANCE.

25/5, Girls Hostel

Government High School

Sector 15,

Chandigarh

15th Nov. 2007

My dear Father

You will be glad to learn that I'm doing very well in my studies. During the last examination, the result of which is out today, I have secured the first position in the aggregate marks.

There are, however, certain problems which I'm facing now. The school authorities have substantially increased the school fees and that quite arbitrary. Then I need a number of books and practical files for which I have no money. I shall, therefore, be grateful if you increase my monthly allowance from the present Rs. 2500/- to 3500/-

Convey my love to Rahul.

Your loving daughter

Priyanka

TO FATHER REQUESTING HIM TO ALLOW YOU TO CONTINUE YOUR STUDIES.

17/14, Ramjas Boys Hostel
Ramjas Public School
New Delhi
5th October, 2008

My dear Father

My examinations are over and I have fared well in all the papers. In your last letter you asked me not to join the next class and return home to lend a helping hand in your business.

I fully understand that our own business is of much more importance than any service which I may join after completing my studies. Dear father, I assure you I have no intention to join any service at all. I too want to join your business a few years later. However, giving up studies at the present moment does not seem proper to me. It is because in the modern world even a businessman is required to be a good communicator. He must also be well-versed in the latest technological innovations. For this, a businessman must at least be a graduate. So, I hope you will kindly allow me to continue my studies to become at least a graduate.

Regards to mamma.

Your loving son

Naresh Bansel

TO FATHER INFORMING HIM OF YOUR PROGRESS IN STUDIES.

78/2, Prashant Vihar
New Delhi.
5th May, 2008
My dear Father

You will be glad to know that I have scored 80% marks in the second Terminal Test. These marks are to be added for the purpose of annual examination. I think I shall top my class. I shall keep alive the family tradition. We have so many toppers in our family. English and Mathematics are my favourite subjects.

They are at my finger's tips. I need not fear Science and Social Studies. I have revised my courses very thoroughly. I have sought the help of all good books. Hindi is my pet subject.Please rest assure, I shall come out with flying colours. I will show excellent results.

My regards to dear Mummy and love to Uday.
With regards,
Your loving son
Kamal Aggarwal

LETTER TO FATHER GIVING HIM HOME NEWS.

15/20A, New Rohtak Road
New Delhi
5th October, 2007

My dear Father

In my last letter I informed you that mother had got her ankle sprained as she fell down while climbing the stairs. She has now fully recovered. Meeta has got the first prize at an inter-school quiz competition and is now puffed up with pride. I am working steadily at my studies and hope to get a good percentage of marks in the final examination. Dear papa, please take care of your health along with business while you are abroad.

With Love.

Your loving daughter

Kamini Malhotra

LETTER TO FATHER TELLING HIM HOW YOU FARED IN THE EXAMINATION.

17/14, Ramjas Boys Hostel
Ramjas Public School
New Delhi
5th October, 2008

My dear Father

My first semester examination is over. You will be glad to learn that I have fared well in all the papers except in Economics. In Mathematics and Accounts I hope to get full marks. In all other subjects, except Economics, I think, I'll get more than 90 per cent marks.

Papa, you'll just laugh when I tell you what I did in Economics. We were asked to draw a graph of birth of girls yearly and I drew a graph of birth of boys yearly instead. Otherwise, I did the paper well. I hope to get about 65 per cent marks in this paper.

With Love.
Yours affectionately
Naresh Singh

LETTER TO YOUR MOTHER COMPLAINING ABOUT THE POOR QUALITY OF FOOD SERVED IN YOUR HOSTEL.

Ramjas Hostel No. 4
Ramjas Public School
Anand Parbat
New Delhi.

Dear mother

I hope that this letter of mine would find you in the best of your health and spirits.

I am aware that you would be very much angry and annoyed with me as I could not write even a single letter to you for more than a month. But I shall tell you the truth. I have suffered three times due to stomach problem. My other colleagues are also not well.

Now, we have been able to analyse the cause of our illnesses. We have come to the conclusion that it is due to the dirty foodstuff, which is being served in the hostel. The contractor of our mess is very careless and cunning. He is playing with the health of the students. The chapatis, which are served to us, are not properly baked. The pulses contain small stones.

In spite of the repeated requests to the contractor for regulating the supply of healthy foodstuff, he is turning a deaf ear. But we have brought this matter to the notice of the principal and the superintendent of the hostel. They have promised to look into our grievances.

I shall inform you about the action and steps taken by him in this regard in my next letter.

Yours' lovingly

Pramood Kumar

LETTER TO MOTHER DESCRIBING THE PRIZE DISTRIBUTION FUNCTION AT YOUR SCHOOL.

25/5, Girls Hostel
Government High School
Sector 15,
Chandigarh
15th February. 2008

My dear Mother

Last Monday was a very exciting day for me. It was because the Annual Prize Distribution Function of our school was held on that day. Ms. Anita Arya, the MLA, was the Chief Guest.

The function was held in our school hall which had been decorated tastefully with balloons and bunting. The Chief Guest arrived on time. The function started at 10 a.m. exact. The President of the school management welcomed the Chief Guest. Then the Cultural Show started. It comprised songs, dances, skits, titbits, histrionics and fancy dress. The audience which included the elite society of the city liked it very much. Thereafter, the Chief Guest gave away the prizes. I got two prizes. Then the Principal read out the achievements of the school during the year. After that the Chief Guest made a short speech. She appreciated the activities of the school on various counts. The function came to an end with the singing of the National Anthem.

Regards to Papa and convey my love to Rohit.

Your loving daughter

Shilini Singh

LETTER TO UNCLE TELLING HIM ABOUT THE PROFESSION YOU WANT TO CHOOSE.

4/14A, Greater Kailash
New Delhi
15th October, 2008

My dear Uncle

In your last letter you asked me about the profession I want to choose. Since I have taken up medical subjects, it is in itself clear that I want to become a doctor.

I know very well that it is very expensive these days to become a doctor. Many Lakhs of rupees are required for this purpose. No doubt, now there are many new courses which are less arduous and more lucrative than those for becoming a highly qualified doctor. But, as you know, I have a special aptitude for this line. And, moreover, my parents can well afford to pay my fees and other expenses.

A doctor can earn a lot these days. At the some time, he can serve humanity by being compassionate, especially to the poor.

I want to both earn and serve but serve more than earn.

My compliments to dear aunt.

Yours affectionately

Ramesh Ahuja

LETTER TO YOUR UNCLE THANKING HIM FOR A GIFT ON YOUR BIRTHDAY.

15/25, Azad Pur
New Delhi
2nd May, 2008.
My dear uncle

My parents celebrated my 12th birthday with great rejoicing. I was heaped with gifts and presents. But the present sent by you was matchless in beauty and utility.

I thank you from the core of my heart for the pretty gift. It gave me great pleasure to receive your lovely gift. It is a very beautiful camera. I will cherish it as a token of your love for me.

The camera is very good and all the members of the family have appreciated the gesture. This shows your deep affection for me.

Kindly pay my regards to dear aunt and sister Neha.

Yours affectionately

Nidhi Aggarwal

LETTER TO YOUR YOUNGER BROTHER WHO IS A BOOK-WORM, ADVISING HIM TO TAKE PART IN GAMES ALSO.

15, Kirti Nagar
New Delhi
15th April , 2008

My dear Gagan,

It pained me to learn that you are always occupied with studies and devote no time to games. Dear, it is not proper.

Overwork will tell upon your health and then you will repent. Remember, "All work and no play makes Jack a dull boy."

You think that times spent in games is wasted. No, it is wrong.

On the contrary, it is gainful. You must bear in mind that games are as useful as studies. They keep us regular, punctual and healthy. They teach us sportsmanship. They widen our circle of friends. Above all, they teach us discipline. A well-educated man with distinction in games has better chances of getting a decent job.

You must find time for games and take active part in them. I believe you will pay heed to my advice.

With love

Your's affectionately

Harish

LETTER TO POSTMASTER AGAINST A POSTMAN.

To

The Postmaster

Gurudwara Road, Karol Bagh

New Delhi

Sir

The postman of our locality does not deserve to be allowed to remain in service. At least, he must be transferred from our locality.

He is not regular in delivering the post. Then he throws the letters, including registered letters, in the open or hands them over to children.

During the last one month, I have lost a number of important letters. Even money order for Rs 5000/- sent to me by my brother from Punjab two months ago hasn't reached me. It seems the postman, Mr. Suresh Bhardwaj, is a pastmaster in the matter of embezzlement. I hope you'll take an early action on my complaint

Thank you.

Yours faithfully

Rakesh Pandit

LETTER TO A SPORTS DEALER FOR SUPPLY OF SPORTS GOODS

To
M/s. Gulati Sports
Jhandewalan Extension
New Delhi.

Sir

I am pleased to inform you that the residents of my colony have recently formed a Sports Club. The Club's Committee has approved of the sports goods as mentioned below.

As a Secretary of the Sports Club I request you to supply us the mentioned articles as early as possible.

Articles	**Quantity**	
Cricket bat	6	
Cricket leather ball	12	Superior
Carrom board	4	(with coins)

Volleyball 4

Kindly send the bills along with the articles through your representative so that we can make the payments.

Thanking you

Yours faithfully

Anil Shrivastav

10/25, Mayur Vihar
New Delhi.
24th May, 2008

LETTER TO THE SPORTS DEALER CANCELLING THE ABOVE ORDER

To

M/s. Gulati Sports

Jhandewalan Extension

New Delhi.

Sir

We had placed an order with you for the supply of sports goods vide our order dated 24th May, 2008. Due to certain unavoidable circumstances we request you to cancel this order for the time being

We hope to place a fresh order in another 35-45 days time. Inconvenience caused to you is regretted.

Thanking you

Yours faithfully

Anil Shrivastav

10/25, Mayur Vihar

New Delhi.

30th May, 2008

LETTER TO SCHOOL FOR BUS SERVICE

The Transport officer
Delhi Public School
Mandir Marg
New Delhi
24th April.,2008

Sir,

Suddenly, the school bus (Route No. D-28) has stopped coming to Munirka Village. Recently, the bus traffic of Munirka Village has been made one way which entails a little longer route. While other school buses have followed the new traffic pattern, our bus (D-28) has preferred to pick up and drop the students outside the Munirka Village i.e. on Mandir Marg causing undue delay and walk of about 1 km.

We shall be obliged if you kindly instruct the bus to continue with the picking up/dropping of the students inside the Munirka Village premises as before. We shall be grateful for your kindness.

Thanking you,
Yours Sincerely
Arvind Kumar

THERE IS AN ADVERTISEMENT FOR THE POST OF TYPIST IN A NEWSPAPER APPLY FOR THE POST GIVING YOUR BIODATA.

To
The Manager
DMS Ltd.
Vishal Nagar
New Delhi

Sub : Application for the post of a typist.

Sir

With reference to your advertisement for the job of typist in 'THE TIMES OF INDIA' dated April 5, I beg to offer my services for the same.

My biodata is as under :

BIO DATA

Name	: Amit Kumar
Father's name	: A.K. Gupta
Age	: 21 Years
Educational Qualifications	: Passed . B. Com.

		exam 2006 in Ist Division
Speed in typewriting	:	60 words per minute
Experience (if any)	:	Worked as a typist to the District Inspector of Schools in a 6 months leave vacancy.

During my school and college career I look active part in all the literary and social activities of the Institutions in which I studied. I also worked as the Editor of the College Magzine.

I attach herewith true copies of my testimonials for your perusal.

I beg to request you to give me an opportunity to serve your organisation. Assuring you a sincere and devoted service.

Thanking you
Yours faithfully
Amit Kumar
12, Budh Vihar
New Delhi

TO A BOOKSELLER ORDERING BOOK.

R.M.S. Public School
Agra
11th December 2007
To
M/s. Maanu Book Depot
Educational Publishers
Pitam Pura
New Delhi-110 034
Dear Sirs

I shall feel obliged if you send me a copy of the following books per V.P.P. at your earliest convenience.

(1) The Advanced Learners Dictionary of Current English.

(2) New English Essays and Letters.

(3) English Course for Secondary Schools, Parts I and II.

Thanking you
Yours truly
Jitender Singh

STORIES

A FOX AND A CROW

Once a hungry fox was moving in the forest in search of food. He wandered here and there, but he could not find anything to eat. At last, he saw a crow. The crow was sitting on the branch of a tree. It had a piece of cheese in its mouth.

The fox saw the cheese and his mouth watered. He hit on a plan. He praised the crow for its sweet voice and prayed to it for singing a song. The crow felt proud and opened his beak for singing. As soon as he opened his mouth, the piece of cheese fell to the ground. The fox ran away with the cheese and ate it up.

☆☆☆

A FOX AND THE GRAPES

Once there was a clever fox. One day, he felt hungry. He went about in search of some food in the forest. He reached a garden. There he saw big bunches of fine ripe grapes. They were hanging from a high vine. His mouth watered at the sight of ripe rapes.

He longed to eat them to his fill. So he jumped. But the vines were too high for him to reach. He jumped many times. But he did not succeed in getting at the grapes. He got tired and left the idea of eating grapes in disgust. But he did not accept defeat. At last he went away saying. These grapes are sour I shall fall ill in case I eat them.

☆☆☆

A HARE AND A TORTOISE

Once upon a time a hare and a tortoise lived in a forest. The hare was very proud of his speed. He thought himself to be the fastest running creature of the forest. The tortoise is a slow walking creature. The hare threw a challenge for a race. The tortoise accepted it. They decided that the crow would work as the referee.

The race began. The hare ran fast and covered three fourth of the distance in no time. He saw a shady tree. He decided to take rest thinking that he would cover the rest of the distance in no time. He slept. The tortoise was walking slowly at his constant speed. He saw the hare sleeping. He passed him. The hare woke up and started running.

It was too late. The tortoise had reached the destination and won the race. Thus the saying, "Slow and steady wins the race" proved to be true.

☆☆☆

A THIRSTY CROW

There was a crow in a village. He was very clever. One hot day, he felt very thirsty. That year, there were no rains. All the rivers and the ponds had gone dry. He flew in search of water. It reached a garden.

He saw a jug of water in a garden. He was overjoyed. But it when began to drink water. He found tnat the level of water in the jug was very low. His beak could not reache it. The crow did not lose heart. It thought of a plan. He collected some pebbles. He threw them one by one in the jug. The water rose up in level.

He quenched his thirst and flew away happily thinking that nothing is impossible in this world.

☆☆☆

HONESTY IS THE BEST POLICY

Once there was a wood-cutter. He used to cut trees in the forest. One day when he was cutting down a tree on the bank of a river, his axe fell down into the river. The river was very deep. He could not take it out. He sat on the bank of the river and began to weep loudly.

God Mercury heard his cries. He asked him the reason of his weeping. The wood-cutter told him the whole story. The God assured him that he would bring out his axe.

He took a dip into the river and came out with a gold axe. The wood-cutter refused to take it because it was not his. Again the God jumped into the water and brought out a silver axe.

The wood-cutter refused to take it telling him that it was not his. Third time the God again jumped into the river and brought out an iron axe.

The wood-cutter happily took it, telling him that the axe was his. God Mercury was very much pleased. He rewarded the wood-cutter with the other two costly axes for his honesty.

★★★

GOD HELPS THOSE WHO HELP THEMSELVES

There was a cartman. One rainy day, he was driving his cart on a muddy road. One of the wheels got stuck up in a mud hole. He tried and tried. He even beat up his bollocks but the cart could not be pulled out. He got disappointed and helpless.

Then he thought of God Herculus. He prayed to him for help. His prayer was sincere and true. So the God appeared there in person. He advised the cartman not to lose heart. He asked him to put his shoulder to wheel. As the cartman did so, the cart moved out of the mud.

The bullocks heaved a sigh of relief. He was equally happy. The God disappeared. But he had taught the cartman that God helps those who help themselves. The moral of the story is trust your hands and put them to work.

☆☆☆

ROBERT BRUCE AND THE SPIDER

Once upon a time there was a king named Robert Bruce. He was defeated in a battle. He was very much disappointed by his defeat. He ran away from the battlefield and thought of finishing his life. He hid himself in a cave so that he might not fall in the hands of the enemy.

A spider lived in the same cave. It was trying to reach the roof of the cave but was slipping down every time. At last it succeeded in its mission. King Bruce was deeply moved by this scene and he decided to make an effort once again. He tried once more and won the battle.

☆☆☆

THE ARAB AND HIS CAMEL

Once an Arab was sleeping in his tent. His camel was lying outside. It was very cold that day. The camel requested the Arab to allow him to cover his neck in the tent. The Arab was a kind man. He allowed him to do so. After some time the camel requested to allow him to put his forelegs in. The Arab agreed. Gradually the camel's entire body was in the tent. It was not a big tent. So the Arab asked the camel to get out. The camel did not listen to him. When the Arab asked the camel again, it grew angry and pushed the Arab out of the tent.

☆☆☆

THE ANT AND THE GRASSHOPPER

In a field one summer's day a Grasshopper was hopping about, chirping and singing to its heart's content. An Ant passed by, hard at work carrying a grain of corn up the ant hill.

"Why not come and play," said the Grasshopper, "instead of working so hard?" "I am storing food for the winter," said Ant, "and recommend you to do the same." "Why bother about winter?" said the Grasshopper; "its summer and food is all around us."

But the Ant went on its way and continued its toil. When the harsh rains of Fall turned to Winter snow the Grasshopper had no food and found itself dying of hunger, while Ant feasted on the corn he had gathered in the summer.

☆☆☆

THE BIRDS, THE BEASTS, AND THE BAT

The birds were constantly fighting with the Beasts, and by turns each won the fight. One time the Birds won and the next time the Beasts won. A Bat, uncertain who would win the fight, always fought on the side which he felt was the strongest. When the Birds and the Beasts finally stopped fighting and became friends they realized that the Bat was a traitor and both the Birds and the Beasts stopped being his friend. And ever since then because of his treachery, the Bat could no longer come out to play during the day, and had to hide in dark scary places, flying always alone and at night.

☆☆☆

THE BLIND MAN WITH A LAMP

It was a dark night. A blind man was walking with a lighted lamp in his hand. Two men laughed at him and asked what use was the lamp to him. The blind man laughed back and said that they were fools. People were generally very careless. They might not notice him in the darkness and bump against him. It was for them that he was carrying a lighted lamp. The two men realised the wisdom of the blind man and apologised to him for laughing at him.

☆☆☆

THE CAP SELLER AND THE MONKEYS

Once a businessman was going to the market to sell his caps. He had a bundle of caps on his back. He was tired. On the way, he saw a shady tree. He thought of taking rest for some time. He put his bundle on the ground and slept.

There were many monkeys living on that tree. They saw the bundle of caps. They came down from the tree. They took the caps one by one and put them on their heads. In the meantime, the businessman woke up. He was very sad to see that his caps were missing. He did not lose heart. He hit upon a plan. He threw his own cap on the ground. The monkeys also did the same. He collected the caps and went away.

☆☆☆

THE CAT AND THE FOX

Once there lived a fox and a cat in a jungle. They always used to boast about his greatness and cleverness. One day the fox told the cat 'You know I am very clever. I know hundreds of tricks so my enemies can not catch me'. For this the cat smiled and said 'I know only one way'.

Just then they heard the loud barks of hunting dogs and saw some men. The cat quickly climbed up the tree and bid in the branches. The fox began to think. He could not decide the way of escape. It was too late. The dogs and men caught and killed the fox.

☆☆☆

THE CRANE AND THE FOX

There was a lake in a dense forest. By the side of the lake there were many big trees. A crane lived on the trees and ate fish in the lake. Also there is a clever fox which lived in the forest. The crane some times shared with the fox the fish it caught in the lake. The both became good friends.

The fox one day thought he would play a joke on his friend. So he said to the crane, "Will you come to dine with me" ? The crane replied, 'Yes friend ! I shall come".

When the crane arrived the fox welcomed the bird warmly. But when they sat to dine, the fox served soup only that too in flat plates.

The fox was able to lap up the whole soup with his tongue easily. But the crane on account of his long bill was not able to drink the soup from the flate plate. The fox had filled his stomach.

He also laughed at the crane for its inability to drink. The crane even though hungry did not show her discomfort. The crane thought "I shall teach the fox a lesson". So one day he said to the fox, "Dear friend, will you please come to dine with me" ? The fox readily agreed to come.

At the dinner the crane also served just soup but in two jugs of long and narrow necks. The crane was able to put the long bill into the jug and drink happily. The fox was not able to drink at all. But licked the jug only from outside. The fox remained hungry. Now it was the crane's turn to laugh at the fox. The fox realised the mistake he committed and cooly went away.

☆☆☆

THREE GREEDY FRIENDS

Once there lived three friends in a village. One day they decided to go to a city to earn their living. They promised to help each other in case of any trouble. On their way, they passed through a thick forest. In the forest, they found a leather bag which was full of gold coins. They were very happy. They decided to divide the coins in three equal parts. They sat down under a tree. By then they felt hungry. One person was sent to buy some food and wine, while the other two stayed behind. The two friends, who stayed behind decided to kill the third friend so that they might have his share for themselves. Mean while, the third friend decided to kill the other two so that he might have all the gold coins. He mixed some poison in the food and returned. The other two killed him as soon as he reached the place. Now the two friend were happy and ate the food. They too died on the spot. Hence the life of the three greedy friends came to an end.

THE DOVE AND THE ANT

In a forest there lived a dove on a tree top by the side of stream. Near the tree there was an ant hill. One day an ant crowled away and fell into the flowing stream. The ant was in great danger. The dove on the tree saw it. The bird dropped a twig near the ant. The ant climbed on the twig.

Soon the twig reached the bank drived by wind. The ant came on the land and was saved.

Some days after a fowler came into the forest. He aimed an arrow at the dove. The fowler was about to release the arrow from his bow. The ant saw the danger to the dove. It came near the fowler and stung deep in his foot. The fowler jerked his foot and lost the aim. The dove flew away unharmed. The life of the dove was saved by the ant.

☆☆☆

THE GREEDY DOG

Once there was a hungry dog. He wandered here and there in search of food. At last he reached the shop of a butcher. He found a piece of meat. He took that piece in his mouth and ran away outside the village.

He reached the bridge of a stream. He saw his own shadow in the water. He thought that there was another dog with a piece of meat in his mouth. He should snatch it. As soon as he opened his mouth his piece fell down into the stream. He lost his own piece of meat and became sorry for his mistake. It is truly said, "Be satisfied with what you have; do not be greedy."

☆☆☆

THE HARE AND THE TORTOISE

One day a hare made fun of the short feet and slow pace of the Tortoise, who replied, laughing: "Though you be swift as the wind, I will beat you in a race." The Hare, thought it was impossible for the turtle to beat him so he accepted the challenge. On the day appointed for the race the two started together. The Tortoise never for a moment stopped, but went on with a slow but steady pace straight to the end of the course. The Hare, quickly ran far ahead of the Tortoise and then decided to lay down for a rest. Laying in the shade along side the road Hare soon fell fast asleep. At last waking up, he sprinted for the finish line but just before he could reach it, the slow moving Tortoise crawled across.

☆☆☆

THE HONEST WOOD CUTTER

One day he was cutting wood from a tree which stood by the side of a big lake. As he cut the branches, his axe slipped and fell into the lake.

The wood cutter was very sad for the loss of his axe and began to weep. The goddes living in the lake felt pity on the wood cutter. She came out of the lake with an axe made of gold and asked him "Is this your axe" ? "No" said the wood cutter, "This is not my axe". Then she showed him a silver axe and said "Is this your axe" ? "No" again the wood cutter said. Finally she showed him the axe made of iron. "Yes, this is my axe!" the wood cutter shouted with joy.

The goddess was much pleased with the honesty of wood cutter. She gave him all the three axes in reward.

☆☆☆

THE LION AND THE MOUSE

Once a lion was sleeping in a forest. A mouse came there. He jumped over the sleeping lion. The lion was disturbed in his sleep. He woke up and caught the mouse in his palm. The mouse trembled on account of fear. He prayed to the lion to show mercy on him. He said that he might be of some help to him some day. The lion laughed but felt pity on the mouse and set him free.

One day some hunters came to that forest. They caught the lion in their net. The lion roared in distress. The mouse heard the roar and came out of his hole. He cut the net and set the lion free. The lion thanked him for his help.

☆☆☆

THE MANAGER AND THE WATCHMAN

The manager of a well-known firm was interviewing applicants for the post of a night watchman he had advertised. It was very difficult to get suitable hand. He always found something wrong in each-one man had brown hair, another had a squint in the left eye, a third was a Jat, fourth too thin, a fifth too fat-another too short, and yet another too tall.

Among the applicants who *came* to the interview for the post there was one Ram Singh. He watched all this as he sat in the verandah patiently awaiting his turn to be interviewed. He resolved to be prepared for anything. When his turn came all went well. The manager found nothing wrong with his appearance, size or constitution. He was so handsome, tall and strong that the manager was really pleased to see such a well-built young man.

'Is your health sound ?" said the manager at last. "No, Sir,' replied Singh, 'not quite. I suffer from one serious complaint'. "What is that" ? said the manager sharply. "Sleeplessness", came prompt reply.

The manager was so pleased with the answer of the young man that, without questioning him further, he engaged him.

☆☆☆

THE SLAVE AND THE LION

The king of a certain country had half a dozen slaves. He treated them harshly. One evening a young slave ran away from his palace.

He escaped into the forest infested with wild animals. Outside a cave, he saw a lion crying in pain. Perhaps it had run into a thorny bush. The beast growled furiously.

He pulled out the thorn from the lion's paw. For a few days it limped. The wound healed and it was all right. A few months later the slave was caught. The king decreed. That the slave be thrown before a hungry lion. It was the severest punishment ever awarded to any offender.

The poor slave was helpless. He was pushed into a lion's cage. The hungry lion roared and leapt from his place. But ıt stoped short and began to lick the slave's feet. It recognised the man and remembered his kindness.

It was the same fellow who had once taken out

the thorn from his paw. The people watched this scene in great amazment. The moral of the story is Good-nees never goes unrewarded.

☆☆☆

THE MONKEY AND THE TRAVELLER

Once a traveller was passing through a thick jungle. He came across a little monkey. He was very ill. The poor animal could not get about. The kind man's heart melted with pity. He carried it on his shoulder wherever he went. He was looked after very tenderly. In the course of time it was all right. It became a constant companion during his journey. At heart, it wanted to repay its saviour. In this way some time passed away.

One day, it was terribly hot. The traveller felt very thirsty. No water could be found thereabout. He became extremely uneasy. This wise animal realized the cause of his restlessness. He quickly climbed up a coconut tree. A few fruits were thrown down. The traveller wasted no time. He broke them, drank the sweet water and quenched his thirst. He thanked the little friend from the bottom of his heart. But for the monkey, the traveller would have breathed his last.

☆☆☆

THE WOLF AND THE LAMB

Once upon a time a lamb was drinking water near the bank of a river. A hungry wolf reached there. Seeing the lamb, his mouth watered. He wanted to kill the lamb. "Why are you making the water muddy ?" he said, The lamb replied respectfully, "Sir the water is flowing down from your side. How can I make it muddy ?" The wolf then said, "Why did you abuse me last year ?" The lamb replied, "But I was not born last year". Now the wolf said. Tour father must have abused me then". Saying these words the wolf tore the lamb to pieces and ate it up.

☆☆☆

TIT FOR TAT

Once there was an elephant called Rammana. It used to go to a river to take a bath. On his way to the river, there was a tailor. The elephant used to put its trunk in the shop. The tailor used to give him some eatable. This continued for some time. Soon they became friends.

One day, the tailor was unwell. He was also mentally upset. As usual the elephant came on its way. He thrust inside the shop expecting some food. But to his surprise and shock, the tailor pricked a needle into his trunk. The elephant felt hurt. It decided to take it out on the tailor.

At the river, it took its bath and then took some muddy water in its trunk. On way back, it again passed the tailor's shop. "Now was the time to take revenge" he thought. And he released the muddy water into the shop there by spoiling new clothes. The tailor suffered a great loss. He had to pay dearly for his rash action.

☆☆☆

TWO FRIENDS AND THE BEAR

Once two friends were going on a long journey. On their way, they had to pass through a dense wood. They promised to help each other on the way. In those days there were no transport. They had to walk through forest, full of dangerous wild animals. When they were passing through the forest, they saw a bear running towards them. One of them knew how to climb the tree. He went up the tree in no time. The other was poor at climbing. He could not find any way to save himself. At last he threw himself on the ground and lay there motionless. When the bear came near him he slopped breathing. The bear sniffed him. He took him for a dead man and went away. When the bear had gone. The friend on the tree came down. He asked his friend who was lying on the ground "What did the bear say in your ear? The letter remembered his friend not coming to his rescue. He replied that the bear had said to him, "Never trust a selfish friend."

TWO CROWS AND A SNAKE

Once upon a time two crows had a nest on a tree. A snake also lived in the hollow trunk of the tree. When the crows flew away in search of food, the snake would eat their eggs. This went on for sometime. The crows then thought out a plan to kill the snake.

There was a river nearby. Many a person came there everyday for bathing. Sometimes the princess also came along with her servants to bath there. As the crows were thinking of their plan, they saw the princess and her servants coming to the river side. The princess soon undressed herself and placed her clothes and ornaments on the bank. She entered the river and had a bath. In the meantime, the crows picked up some ornaments and flew away. The servants saw this and followed the crows. They dropped ornaments into the hollow trunk.

When the princess came out of the river, she

found her ornaments lost. She ordered her servants to search for her ornaments. When the servants reached the tree, they saw a snake near the ornaments. They at once killed it with their sticks and took the ornaments. Then they went back to the river.

Thus the clever crows took revenge on their enemy. They lived in peace thereafter.

☆☆☆

UNION IS STRENGTH

Once there was an old father. He had three sons. They did not love one another. Their father was upset. He often advised them to live peace and not to quarrel. But they were very obstinate.

One day the old man got sick. He lay on his death bed. He was worried about his sons. He called them and asked them to bring a bundle of sticks. They immediately obeyed him and brought a bundle. Then he asked them one by one to try to break the bundle. None of them could do so. He asked them to untie the bundle. There after he asked them to break all sticks. All the three could easily break the sticks.

The sons understood the message. So long as the sticks were tied together, they could not break them. So if they lived untidely, nobody will be able to harm them. They followed their old father's advice and learnt that union is strength.

☆☆☆